Ace Books by William Shatner

TEKWAR
TEKLORDS
TEKLAB
TEK VENGEANCE

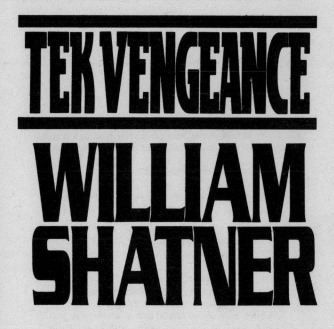

TEK VENGEANCE

WILLIAM SHATNER

ACE BOOKS, NEW YORK

This Ace Book contains the complete text of the original hardcover edition. It has been completely reset in a typeface designed for easy reading, and was printed from new film.

TEK VENGEANCE

An Ace Book/published by arrangement with the author

PRINTING HISTORY
Ace/Putnam edition/January 1993
Ace edition/December 1993

ISBN: 0-441-80012-2

ACE®
Ace Books are published by The Berkley Publishing Group,
200 Madison Avenue, New York, NY 10016.
ACE and the "A" design are trademarks
belonging to Charter Communications, Inc.

10 9 8 7 6 5 4 3 2 1

Acknowledgments

Carmen La Via, my long-time friend and agent,
   who encourages me to write and write and
   write and write;
Ron Goulart, my friend and literary guru;
Ivy Fischer Stone, Fifi Oscard, also agents, also
   friends;
Mary Jo Fernandez, my assistant, who tells me
   what page I'm on;
Susan Allison, my laser-eyed editeer.

— 1 —

THE MAN WHO found out what was going to happen didn't get the time to tell anyone about it. They killed him before he could pass along what he had learned.

That happened in Berlin, just at dawn, on a chill, misty day in the spring of the year 2121. He was a tall, lanky man in his late thirties. His name doesn't matter.

He got back to his flat on a narrow street near the Kemperplatz as the morning light was beginning to show at the panes of colored glass in the leaded windows of the bedroom.

The woman he was living with was already awake, sitting on the edge of their old-fashioned fourposter bed. Wearing a white robe, she was in the process of tying back her long blonde hair with a strand of black ribbon.

The dawn light touched at her pretty face as she smiled up at him.

He crossed the room, feeling safe and secure. And happy that he'd found someone like her.

Leaning, he kissed her on the cheek. The instant his lips touched her flesh, there was an enormous explosion.

The force of it ripped him to pieces, tore the wall of the bedroom into jagged chunks, smashed every window into thousands of glittering shards, threw what was left of him down toward the grey, misty street below.

The woman was destroyed, too. The metal frame of her body, the plastic skin, the intricacy of wires and tubes, chips and circuitry were scattered across the new day by the violence of the explosive charge that had been hidden inside her.

Everything mixed and tangled together— flesh, blood, mortar, wire, metal—as it flew free of the exploding room and fell down through the greyness of the morning.

So the agent never got to make his report to the International Drug Control Agency. If he had, somebody there would probably have told Jake Cardigan.

And because of that Jake's life was going to change, profoundly. But he had no premonition of that, no notion of the darkness that lay ahead.

His troubles began, although Jake wasn't aware of it at the time, on a warm, clear afternoon on that same day in the early spring of 2121.

As the agency skycar approached the Seawall Commercial Complex in the Santa Monica Sector of Greater Los Angeles, Sid Gomez said, "We're arriving at our destination, *amigo.*"

Jake, a goodlooking, though weatherbeaten, man of near fifty, was slouched in the passenger seat. "So I notice."

Below on Landing Lot #3 rose up a 100-foot-high replica of the torchbearing arm of the Statue of Liberty. It was trimmed with throbbing crimson neon tubing and above the flaming torch floated, in 5-foot-high letters, the words NEWS AND TRUTH alternating with GLA FAX-TIMES. At the edge of the lot loomed the impressive 20-story newspaper building, constructed of silvery metal and panels of multicolored real glass.

Hunching slightly, Gomez punched out a landing pattern on the control panel. "You've been somewhat melancholy thus far today. You brooding about something?"

Jake replied, "I suppose I am, yeah."

"Would the topic be Beth Kittridge?"

The skycar circled the elbow of the neon-trimmed arm once and then settled into a space near its base. A few dozen yards away the foamy surf of the Pacific Ocean was hitting at the rocky beach.

Jake said, "I don't like the idea of Beth's having to go over to Berlin next week."

Gomez was a dark, curlyhaired man, ten years younger than his partner. "From the scraps of information you've brought back after visiting the lady up in NorCal, I gather she doesn't much favor the jaunt herself."

"That trip is going to be damn dangerous for her, risky." Unhooking his safety gear, Jake eased out of the vehicle.

His partner joined him on the grey lot surface. "The International Drug Control Agency is going to be looking after her," he said. "You're going along, too. Beth'll be safe."

Jake shrugged his left shoulder, thrusting his fists deep into his trouser pockets. "The Teklords are a vengeful bunch," he said. "Right now they're not especially fond of Beth—nor of me."

The two of them started walking along an illuminated pathway. It led them across the landing lot, through a plastiglass door and into a large foyer. As the door whispered shut behind them, the sound of the ocean died and unobtrusive string music swiftly surrounded them.

Directly ahead a large viewscreen rose up silently through a thin floor slot. The face of a very handsome blond man appeared, smiling. "Welcome to the Executive Wing of the *GLA Fax-Times*," he greeted in a deep, booming voice. "I am obliged by SoCal state law to inform you that I am nothing more than an electronically generated composite image and not, in point of fact, a real person."

"Don't feel bad," consoled Gomez. "I'm a real person and there are a lot of disadvantages."

"Ha ha," said the image. "Well, enough good-natured kidding, gentlemen. Please—Mr. Cardigan first—enter the ID Booth and allow us to check your ret patterns and fingerprints."

Jake obliged, stepping into the cubicle to the left of the screen.

"Name? Affiliation? Destination?" requested the booth out of its soundbox.

"Jake Cardigan. I'm an operative with the Cosmos Detective Agency," he answered. "An editor of yours, Miss China Vargas, wants to see us."

"Look into the eyeslots and at the same time press your hands, both of them, to the recogplates. Thank you."

Jake complied.

After exactly eleven seconds the booth announced, "Yes, you're Jake Cardigan."

"Thanks," said Jake. "That's good to know."

"You can, as soon as your associate has been cleared, enter Doorway #5 and proceed to the Executive Dining Area."

After Gomez established the fact that he was Gomez, the two detectives used the indicated doorway and then started down a curving ramp.

"Do you think," inquired Gomez, "that I'd do better with women if I had blond wavy hair?"

"Doubtful. Besides, how can you possibly do better than you're doing now?"

"*Es verdad.* You can't top perfection."

The Executive Dining Room was large and below the sea. Through the wide tinted windows the ocean of the Santa Monica Sector coast could be seen, rich with flickering marine life.

At a table beside a seaview window sat a broadshouldered silverhaired young man and a slim young woman. They watched Jake and Gomez for a moment and then the woman, who was completely bald and wore a crimson business suit, stood up.

She came striding over and halted about five feet away. Hands on hips, she scrutinized them.

"Shit," she said finally, "I didn't think you guys would be this old."

⸺ 2 ⸺

CHINA VARGAS HAD a small tattoo of a spread-winged raven on her gleaming hairless head. She rubbed at it thoughtfully with her forefinger as she gazed across the lunch table at them. "Shit, I don't know," she said to the young man with silvery hair. "Do you think they're up to handling this, Larry hon? It's liable to be, you know, strenuous."

Larry Knerr scowled. When he shrugged, the fur-trimmed lapels of his suitcoat brushed at his earlobes. "I've already told you, China, that I can do this particular chore without any—"

"Maybe," suggested Jake as he slowly rose up out of his chair, "you'd better start over again with a different detective agency, Miss Vargas."

"But I can't," she complained, sighing. "What I mean is, you're the one who was specifically requested."

Knerr, who was an Associate Field Editor of the Fax-Times Newsyndicate, said, "No one apparently realized what sorry shape Cardigan is in these days. Leave him on the bench, China, and let me and my crew do the job."

"You know I'm not—"

"Besides, the guy has a terrible rep," the silverhaired editor pointed out. "He's an excon, for one thing. He has a foul temper, an exwife who's in the jug because of fraternizing with Tek biggies and—"

"Do we," Gomez inquired of their hostess, "absolutely need Mr. Knerr in our little discussion group?"

"Not exactly, no. Except Larry is in charge of our Latin America desk and so—"

"Mightn't he," continued Gomez amiably, "be happy taking a stroll along the beach? He might perhaps skip pebbles across the pounding surf and commune with the gulls."

"Well, I suppose we don't truly need him to—"

"Wait a flaming minute." Knerr glared at Gomez. "I'm a major exec with this organization. If anybody is going to take his leave, buddy, you—"

"I'll escort you to the exit." Smiling thinly, Gomez arose.

"Like hell you will." Knerr's chair fell over backwards as he jumped to his feet.

Jake walked around the table, took hold of the man's left arm and twisted it up behind his back. With his other hand he caught the fur collar. "It would be a good idea to depart right now," he advised. "When Gomez starts smiling like that, it—"

"All right, okay." Knerr tried to wiggle free. "I'm not one to force my company on anyone. Although, China, I really think you're making a mistake in dealing with these superannuated gumshoes. Especially since—"

"Mr. Knerr is leaving us now." Jake escorted the struggling editor across the underwater room and let him go near the door.

"It's not smart to antagonize the media, Cardigan," warned Knerr as he pushed out of the room.

Back at the table Jake asked China, "Are you ready to talk about why you wanted to hire us?"

"Shit, yes," she answered. "Sit down, will you? Larry annoys lots of people. Most of them ignore him, but some, like you, prefer to toss him out on his ear."

Gomez, both elbows resting on the table top, said, "Walt Bascom, our boss at Cosmos, didn't give us too many details on this case. Suppose—"

"It isn't *my* case. Until my father, who's the

9

publisher of this rag, stuck me with this job, I'd never heard of Will Sparey."

"Will Sparey?" Frowning, Jake sat down again. "What's he got to do with this?"

"Will Sparey *is* the case. What I mean is, you two guys have to go down to Brazil, locate him and bring him safely home. That's not my idea, but my father insists we owe it to Sparey."

"Sparey disappeared ten or eleven years ago down there," said Jake. "Nobody's heard of him since."

"Until now," said the bald young woman.

Gomez said, "He was a war correspondent for this very paper, wasn't he?"

"Yeah, he was covering the final Brazil War, when he vanished somewhere in the back country," answered Jake. "We were pretty good friends, during the days when I was a cop with the SoCal State Police."

"That must've been before you and I teamed up. I don't think I ever met—"

"Are you gents through reliving the past?"

Jake narrowed his left eye. "What happened to your hair?"

"I had it electrically removed. Baldness is very much in fashion. Among *younger* people."

He said, "Has Sparey contacted you?"

"Not him, his damn daughter."

"Jean Marie?"

"I guess so. How many daughters did he have?"

"Just one."

"Well, then that's who. Skinny black girl of about twenty."

"Twenty." Jake glanced out a viewindow. "Yeah, I guess she'd be at least that by now. Is she here in Greater LA?"

"No, down in Rio de Janeiro, Brazil. Dying."

"This hasn't been a wellwrought briefing up to now," mentioned Gomez. "Perhaps you can back up some, *chiquita,* and provide us with more details on the various—"

"Don't call me *chiquita,*" warned China. "I hate Mexicanisms. Simply because my father is originally from across the border doesn't mean—"

"Get back to Jean Marie Sparey." Jake leaned forward and tapped her arm. "What's wrong with her?"

China tilted her bald head to the left. "She's dying, Cardigan. I'm not certain from what," she answered. "Look, the point is she got in touch with my father yesterday, claimed she knows where her long-lost dad is. My father, being overly sentimental about just about everyone but me, feels he's got to finance your trek down there to Brazil to find this oldtime *Fax-Times* reporter and haul him back to civilization."

Jake said, "Hell, your paper has reporters and correspondents scattered all over the world. Why don't you just have somebody who already works for you locate Sparey?"

When China shook her head, the wings of the

raven seemed to flutter. "Shit, Cardigan, it isn't that easy. This Anna Marie—is that her name?"

"Jean Marie."

"Yeah, her. She refuses to tell us exactly where Will Sparey is at the moment." Deep annoyance showed on China's face. "She insists, and my halfwit father is humoring her, that she won't confide in anyone but you." The young editor's nose wrinkled. "She even calls you Uncle Jake."

Shaking his head, Jake told her, "I won't be able to head down to Rio until I get back from Berlin next week."

"Hey, no. You have to go right now, as soon as possible."

"Why is that?"

"The girl," replied China, "isn't expected to live more than a few days."

— 3 —

BASCOM HAD THE viewalls of his large cluttered office atop Tower II of the Cosmos Detective Agency Building blanked. Nothing of the afternoon Laguna Sector outside showed and the whole place had a dim twilight feel to it. "Did I mention the fee?" he asked Jake as he halted in his zigzag pacing.

"Yeah. It's large."

"Extremely so," agreed the agency head. "Alfonso Vargas is rich. He wants Will Sparey found and brought back to the bosom of the *Fax-Times* and he's willing to pay handsomely. Cosmos will profit, you two gents will profit."

Gomez was perched on the edge of one of the metal desks. "I can go to Brazil right away," he volunteered. "Then, soon as Jake is through in Berlin, he can join me down there."

13

"The Sparey child," reminded Bascom, "won't confide in anyone except Jake himself."

"I can phone her." Jake was hunched in a fat armchair. "I'll explain that Gomez is even more trustworthy than I am and that she can tell him what she knows."

Bascom, a small rumpled man in his middle fifties, gave a brisk shake of his head. "This lass is at death's door," he said. "Her team of doctors and quacks confirms the fact that she's too ill to carry on a phone conversation with anyone, even her dear old Uncle Jake."

"I thought," said Jake, "she phoned the *Times* yesterday."

"Naw, she had one of her medics from the São Jose Private Hospital do that. On top of which, she's in even worse shape today than she was yesterday. Do enough Tek, pretty soon you don't care about much else. Her immune system's probably been shot for months, so the tiniest bug could have done her in any time. Sinking fast, is what the poor kid is doing. They seem surprised she's lasted this long."

Jake stretched up out of the chair. "You know how I feel about Beth," he told his boss. "She has to leave for Berlin in just four days to testify at her father's trial at the World Drug Court and—"

"Jake, I've already assured you that the IDCA boys won't let any harm come to her." Bascom started to pace among the piles of fax-memos and stacks of microfiles that dotted the carpeting. "Granted, they aren't quite as efficient as Cosmos operatives, but they'll have all kinds of extra security people going along just to protect Beth." He slowed, halted. "Since the Drug Court has charged her daddy with being in cahoots with the Teklords, she's the only honest soul left who can work on completing the Kittridge anti-Tek system."

"That's exactly why the Tek cartels want her dead."

"But it's also why the drug agency boys will make damn sure no harm comes to her," insisted Bascom. "They may not feel about Beth the way you do, Jake, but that anti-Tek system is vital to them."

"Nevertheless, I still intend to go along with her," said Jake evenly. "There's no way I can travel to Rio, interview Jean Marie and then go hunting for Sparey. Not in the few days I have."

"Unless the *hombre* happens to be holed up within walking distance of that Rio hospital," said Gomez.

"That'd be the only way we could find him fast enough for me to get back here in time."

"Shall I remind you that you're a fulltime employee of this agency?" inquired Bascom, eyeing Jake. "Would that have any effect in persuading you to take this case?"

"I have to go with her on this trip to Berlin. If you want to fire me, well, then maybe—"

"I'm not suggesting that. But, damn it, Jake, this is an important case for us. The fee is nice and we can probably get other lucrative jobs out of the paper. On top of which, Will Sparey is one of your dearest buddies and—"

"We were friends," acknowledged Jake. "And, sure, I knew Jean Marie when she was a kid. Any other time, I'd head straight for Rio."

Bascom contemplated the distant grey ceiling. "You better take a look at something."

Gomez said, "I sense a dirty trick coming."

"Not at all, nope," the chief assured them. "However, earlier today Vargas sent over a vidcaz." He took three steps ahead, then three back, studying his feet all the while. "It's quite heartbreaking, Jake, so I've been debating whether or not even to—"

"A vidcaz of what?"

"Apparently Jean Marie Sparey summoned up enough strength sometime yesterday, poor little thing, to gasp out a brief message to you. You don't have to watch it, but . . ."

Jake rubbed his palms together slowly. "Okay," he said, "let's see the damn thing."

The young woman stretched out on the hospital bed was gaunt, with deep shadows underscoring her eyes and her cheekbones. Her wasted body was hooked up, by way of an intricacy of twisting tubes and curling wires, to a complex assortment of glittering medical gadgets that surrounded her white servobed.

"That's Jean Marie Sparey." Bascom nodded at the large vidwall screen.

"Christ," said Jake, "what's wrong with her?"

"She'll explain."

Jean Marie's skeletal right hand began to flutter. Finally she touched the control panel on the frame of the bed. The bed made a whirring sound and elevated her to a near sitting position.

"I . . . sure hope . . . that this reaches you . . . Uncle Jake," the young woman said in a thin, faraway voice. "You don't mind . . . my calling you . . . Uncle Jake, do you . . . the way I used to?"

Jake moved closer to the screen.

Jean Marie continued in her faint voice, "They're letting me make this . . . I sure hope . . . you can come see me . . . Uncle Jake . . . I'm a real mess, huh? It's . . . it's mostly from doing Tek . . . had a lot of seizures and . . . I really . . . truly . . . futzed up my body and . . . anyway, please . . . I must . . . talk to you."

Jake was only a few feet from the image of the dying girl.

"My father is . . . alive . . . and I can tell you how to . . . get to him . . . I want to . . . see him again . . . before . . . well, you understand, Uncle Jake . . . You can bring him here to me . . . but there isn't . . . much time . . ." Her eyelids flickered, then drifted shut.

Someone unseen said, "Very well, that's enough."

"No, I have to convince Uncle Jake to come
. . . he's the only one I can trust . . ."

"I'm sorry, we must stop."

The big screen went blank.

"Just as I said," murmured Bascom, clearing
his throat. "Heartbreaking."

Jake turned toward him. "Okay, I'll go see
her," he said, his voice not quite under control.
"And I'll get the search for her father started."

"Good, that's fine."

"But I have to be back here in Greater LA in
time to go to Berlin with Beth."

Bascom nodded. "I'll guarantee you that," he
said.

═ 4 ═

JAKE WAS IN the bedroom, absently packing a suitcase, when his son came home to the new seaside condo they shared in the Malibu Sector. It was late afternoon.

He heard something fall over and something smash. Calling, "Dan, what's happening?" he ran down the hall to the living room.

Dan, a lanky young man of fifteen, was standing in the center of the bright room. He was scowling down at a small tipped over plastable and the broken voxclock lying sprawled beside it.

"Hi, Dad." He came over to hug Jake.

Jake returned the hug. "So?"

"I kicked over the table."

"Any particular reason?"

"I was pissed off about something." He dropped his school gear on the low white sofa. "Sorry."

"Something I ought to know about?"

"Not really, no." Dan unfastened his SoCal State Police Academy tunic, slipped out of it and tossed it in the direction of the sofa. "I didn't expect you to be home this early."

"You wouldn't have booted the furniture if you'd known I was around, huh?"

"Probably not, nope."

Jake put a hand on his son's shoulder. "C'mon—what's wrong, Dan?"

Moving away from him, Dan bent and righted the table. "It was just a thing that happened in one of my classes at the academy today," he said. "I . . . well, I suppose you'll hear about it."

"It'll spoil the surprise," said Jake, sitting on the sofa, "but you might as well fill me in now."

Dan gathered up the clock, depositing the remains on the uprighted table. "Do you know an asshole named Dick Farber?"

"Sure, we were SoCal State cops together. Back when," he answered. "Dick and I, though, were never what you'd call close friends."

"I deduced as much," said his son. "Farber was a guest lecturer in our Interrogation Procedures class this afternoon. When the TA-bot gave him the roster and he saw my name, he wanted to know if I was related to you. I said you were my father and . . . Well, he made some remarks."

"About my having spent time as a prisoner up in the Freezer?"

"That was one of the topics. Farber thinks you were guilty of Tek dealing." Dan's hands fisted at his sides. "He hinted, you know, that if it hadn't been for the influence of corrupt people like Bascom you'd still be on ice up there."

"Even though I was cleared of all those charges after I got out, you're still going to run into people who'll tell you I was really guilty," he told his son. "Farber's one of them."

"I know," said Dan. "You warned me when I first told you I wanted to go into police work, that there'd be cops who don't think much of you. And, since they didn't care for you, they probably weren't going to be too nice to me."

"Looks like that's turning out to be so. Why is the academy going to contact me?"

"Oh, because they have a halfassed rule about cadets punching teachers. Even guest lecturers."

Jake grinned. "You hit Farber?"

Dan poked at his own midsection. "Right here. Twice."

Getting up, Jake said, "Okay, I'll have a talk with a couple of the people I know at the academy."

"You don't have to fight my battles. I just wanted you to know what—"

21

"Farber was out of line, too, Dan. I'll get this straightened out. Okay?"

"Sure, okay. Thanks, Dad."

"This probably won't affect your standing at school. But, hey, don't slug any more of my former colleagues."

"Try not to. But that asshole made me mad."

"I understand." Jake moved toward the hall. "I'll be leaving in about an hour. Going up to Berkeley to see Beth."

"Has something happened?"

"Not to Beth, but Gomez and I have to leave for Rio de Janeiro early tomorrow. I want to see Beth, spend some time with her, before I go."

"Rio?"

Jake outlined the new Cosmos assignment to his son, explaining why he felt obliged to go down there to Brazil.

When he finished, Dan told him, "I can see why you feel you have to do this."

"Yeah, except this isn't the right time."

"If I know you, you'll find this Sparey quickly."

"Maybe," said Jake. "The thing is— Oh, hell."

"What?"

"Nothing." Jake shook his head.

"No, you look like something's worrying you."

"Only a feeling," said Jake. "A feeling that I should stay with Beth and not let her out of my sight."

— =5= —

IT WAS RAINING in the hills above Berkeley, a quiet persistent rain that fell straight down through the deepening twilight. The beams of the landing lights of Jake's skycar cut through it, illuminating the black surface of the parking rectangle next to Beth's hillside cottage.

He set the skycar down, remained in the driveseat.

From out the speaker on his dash came a voice. "You've passed primary clearance, Mr. Cardigan," it announced. "Now, if you would, please, exit your vehicle. Remain standing beside it with your hands clasped behind your neck."

Jake complied. The darkening night was cold, the rain hitting at him was chill.

From a kiosk at the edge of the landing area came a copperplated robot. "Good evening, Mr. Cardigan," he said. "As you're aware, these security procedures serve to—"

"Honestly, Desmo, you know it's Jake as well as I do." Beth, a rain cape draped over her slim shoulders, had come running out a side door of her cottage.

Jake smiled at her. "It's okay," he said.

"All this rigamarole," complained the pretty, darkhaired young woman. "It really gives me a pain in several strategic locations."

"I'm sorry, Miss Kittridge," apologized Desmo/1343-K. "Yet we all have to follow certain—"

"What's the fracas about?" A tall black man, carrying a plas umbrella and a drawn lazgun, stepped through the hedge surrounding the parking area. "Oh, hi, Jake."

"Evening, Emmett."

Beth turned to the International Drug Control Agency man. "We all know this is Jake," she said. "I was simply trying to save some time."

Emmett Neal frowned at her. "I'd appreciate it, Beth, really now, if you'd let us do our job without—"

"Go ahead," Jake invited the robot. "Check me out."

Beth, making an impatient noise, folded her arms. "Okay, run your tests and establish, beyond a shadow of a doubt, that Jake is actually Jake."

The copperplated robot quickly checked Jake's retinal patterns, his fingerprints and his DNA-ID. "He's Jake Cardigan," he announced, stepping back.

"No kidding?" Beth laughed, taking hold of Jake's arm. "May I drag him inside now, Emmett?"

"Sure, Beth. Just keep in mind that all this red tape serves an import—"

"I know. Forgive me for butting in." Squeezing Jake's arm, she led him inside her warm, bright cottage.

He kissed her one more time. "I've missed you."

They were standing in the parlor, her fallen rain cape lying at their feet.

She said, "It's only been a week."

"That can be a hell of a long time."

"Yes, I know. I often wish they'd let me work at a lab closer to Greater LA." Putting her hands on his shoulders, she moved a step back from him. "Is there something wrong?"

"Nothing beyond what I told you on the vidphone."

"You seem sad."

"I'm not sad," he assured her, attempting a grin. "Never am when I'm with you."

"I understand why you have to go to Brazil," she said. "And since you'll be back before I have to leave, there's really nothing to worry about."

Jake pulled her closer to him again. "Could be this has to do with my getting older," he admitted. "I'm feeling very vulnerable lately and I worry about the people I love—you, Dan, Gomez. Worry that something terrible is going to happen to you."

"Eventually something terrible happens to everybody," she said. "You've got to get over the notion, however, that your main purpose in life is to keep that from occurring. It's much too big a job, Jake."

"I suppose."

"I was going to suggest that we have dinner now—but why don't we go to bed first?"

"A fine idea," he said.

Through the oneway viewindow of the parlor you could see down across the rainswept city to the San Francisco Bay beyond. The lights of Berkeley and of the craft on the bay were blurred by the rain.

Jake rested his cup of neocaf on the table next to the sofa he was sharing with Beth. "I suppose there's no way you can get out of going to Berlin?"

"My father's on trial for selling out to Sonny Hokori and some other choice Teklords," she reminded him. "I'm a major witness, not somebody they're going to excuse."

"Even so, I'd—"

"There's no use postponing things. I want to get this over with," she told him. "Once my part in the trial is done with, I can get back here to the lab and finish up my work on the anti-Tek system."

"How close are you to finishing?"

"Hopefully just a few weeks."

"After that you can come back to Greater LA."

"That's what I'm counting on."

Standing, Jake walked over to the window. "If only this damn Brazil job hadn't come up."

"You wouldn't feel right if you didn't go help the Sparey girl."

"That's the line Bascom used on me, but his motives aren't exactly pure."

"Sure, he's crass. He's also right this time, though."

Jake nodded.

Beth said, "Keep in mind that you'll be back in plenty of time to make the trip with us."

"Us?"

She laughed. "I mean with me and Agents Neal, Griggs and McBernie," she said, "plus the rest of the IDCA security people the IDCA has assigned to looking after me."

"Do you really have faith in these guys? In their ability to protect you?"

Leaving the sofa, she moved to his side. "They can be bothersome, but they're efficient," she said. "Is there something you know that you're not telling me?"

"Nothing, nope."

"You act as though you've heard about somebody's plot to do me harm."

He grinned, shaking his head. "It's only that I love you. That makes me worry about what might happen."

She caught hold of his hand. "Okay, we both know what the Tek cartels are capable of," she said. "But keep in mind, okay, that I'm also not bad at taking care of myself. You ought to know that by now."

"I do, yeah," he said. "I seem to be developing mother hen instincts. That's what you get for letting an aging cop into your life."

Smiling, she said, "From now on let me do the worrying."

Toward dawn, when thin grey light began to show at the curved ceiling panels high above the bed, Jake woke up.

During the night Beth had moved away from his side and was now sleeping near the opposite edge.

Jake's mouth was dry and there was a tightness across his chest. Watching Beth, he tried to recall the dream that had frightened him into waking. But he couldn't recapture any details, only a blurred remembrance of being somewhere that was filled with an awful silence.

He sat up, continuing to watch the sleeping young woman. She was breathing evenly, lying with the right side of her face against the pillow and her fisted hand pressed to her chin. Her bare left shoulder rose and fell gently.

"I love you, Beth," he said quietly.

Then, leaning, he kissed her on the shoulder. She murmured softly, but didn't awaken.

—=6=—

As the Passaro Airways skyliner went climbing up through the morning, Gomez said,
"Well, I think it's important."

"Not to me." Jake was occupying the window
seat.

His partner leaned slightly out into the aisle,
eyes narrowing. "You're not using the old
cabeza," he said. "Whether the lovely lady attendant assigned to our section of this airship
is an android or a true human—that's *muy im-
portante*."

"To you."

"Okay, say that the lovely ravenhaired lass
yonder is indeed an android," continued
Gomez, watching her. "Then, which is not
beyond the realm of possibility, especially con-

sidering the way she's been eyeing me and simpering from the moment I stepped aboard, suppose that she and I arrange a rendezvous in Rio de Janeiro—after, of course, I've diligently helped you clean up the Sparey business. And suppose further that my current wife finds out about it and asks for a divorce. I'd hate, *amigo,* to have my marriage go flooey just because I shacked up with a machine."

"If that flight attendant were an android, Sid, she'd have to wear a tag identifying her as such. It's the law."

"It could've fallen off."

"Unlikely."

"Or suppose the lass is a kamikaze, one of those assassinating andies so favored by the Tek gangs? If I were to give her nothing more than a cordial, avuncular pat on the backside— *kapow!* We explode and probably blow an unsightly hole in the side of this crate."

"You ought to bring stuff to read on these trips," suggested Jake, slouching further in his seat. "That would distract you, keep you from fantasizing."

"You have to admit she has flawless skin."

"Didn't notice."

"And perfect hair."

"You can buy perfect hair at any mall."

"To me she seems much too attractive to be a mere human."

"Next time she passes, ask her."

"Questions like that are difficult to put."

"Well, at least spare me further speculations."

Gomez sighed. "It's tough having an obtuse partner."

"Meaning?"

"That the purpose of this sparkling dialogue, *amigo*," admitted his partner, "has been to lift you out of the glum mood I find you in."

"I'm not glum."

"No? You'd have to brighten up considerably before you could even get hired as a professional mourner."

Jake straightened up. "Shows, huh?"

"You having trouble with Beth?"

"Everything was fine in Berkeley."

"Then you must be worrying that some of our Tek buddies will try to hurt her."

Jake said, "You've been married several times."

"*Verdad,* although beside the point."

"I was married once." Jake looked out at the bright morning sky. "The—well, you know all about Kate. Point is, I think I'm ready to try again."

"*Bueno.* You can't do better than Beth."

"Sure, but I think she can do better than me."

"Not unless I was available."

Jake said, "I'm going to be fifty."

"That happens to us all—unless we shake hands with a kamikaze or otherwise cash in our chips prematurely."

"Beth isn't even thirty."

"That's not an immense gap. Besides which, she obviously loves you."

"There's Dan to take into consideration, too."

"Trust me, Jake, your son likes her and she likes him," his partner assured him. "Soon as you two are back in Greater LA, go fetch a preacher. I'll do the best man chores."

Jake grinned. "It's a deal," he said.

The highly polished silver bellbot stepped over to the living room's high, wide viewindow. The window was blanked. "And what view would you like, *senhor?*" he asked Gomez, silvery fingers hovering over the control panel.

"How about just what's out there?"

"Ah, but the Hotel Maravilha offers no less than twenty-five exceptional views, brought to you by our exclusive skycam system," explained the robot. "There is, for example, an absolutely stunning view of Sugar Loaf. Or you and your associate might prefer gazing on the famous immense statue of Christ that adorns—"

"We'll take care of it," Jake told him. "You can go now."

"There is also, for the politically minded, a twenty-four-hour view of our perennial president, General Silveira, delivering choice—"

"Depart," advised Gomez, nodding in the direction of the door.

"I'll leave you with this one." The bellbot

touched a button. "An awesome vista of Ipanema Beach complete with a bevy of—"

"So long," said Gomez.

"*Adeus*. Enjoy the view—and your stay at the Maravilha."

Gomez switched the window to *Actual View*. "Our actual view seems to be a stunning vista of the wall across the way."

"Well, enjoy it," said Jake. "I'm heading for the São Jose Private Hospital."

Gomez turned his back to the view. "I've worked on cases in Rio before," he said. "While you're calling on the ailing Jean Marie, I'll contact some of my erstwhile informants and pay a few calls. Meet you back here at nightfall at the latest."

Jake headed for the door. "Be discreet."

"I'm incapable of anything else," his partner assured him.

— 7 —

On the side of the 5-story building that Jake was passing was mounted a 3-story-high vidscreen. Showing on it was a huge image of General Silveira, wearing an impressive, glittering blue and gold uniform. A short, pudgy man in his late fifties, the ruler of Brazil was striding back and forth on an ornate elevated dais addressing a massive crowd of enthusiastic, cheering citizens. The general's words came booming out of a multitude of speakers, some mounted on the building and some floating over the afternoon street.

Slowing, Jake stopped and gazed up at the Portuguese politician. He stood there, looking up and seemingly taking in the general's speech, for over a minute.

Then, without looking behind him, Jake continued along the Avenida General Silveira. At the next corner he turned onto a side street. Sprinting, dodging pedestrians, he slipped into an alley alongside the Carmen Miranda Museum.

Jake pressed his back to the mosaic tiles of the museum wall, watching the people passing. "Let's talk," he suggested, stepping out and grabbing the arm of the broadshouldered young man who'd been following him.

"I beg your blinking pardon?"

Jake yanked him into the alley, spun him around and pushed him front first against the wall. "Start off by explaining why you're tailing me."

Larry Knerr scowled. "How the hell did you tumble that I was?"

"I don't know," said Jake with a shrug. "Maybe it was the sun glinting on your silvery hair, maybe it was a glimpse of your fetching skyblue suit."

"Actually, Cardigan, I'm simply working."

"At what?"

"Could you, do you think, cease grinding me into this blinking wall?"

Letting go of him, Jake stepped back. "So?"

"I'm a newsman, remember? This is a story, probably a big one."

"No, this isn't a story at all," Jake told the *Fax-Times* syndicate editor. "This is a job that

China Vargas' father hired Cosmos to handle.
A job that requires privacy, not limelight."

"Well, hell, Cardigan." Knerr brushed dust
off his skyblue coat. "I work for the Vargas
family, too, you know. And, shit, this job you're
on has the makings of a tophole yarn, something our—"

"Where are you staying?"

"At the Hotel Triunfo."

Jake advised, "Go back there."

"You can't simply order a newsman off a—"

"Otherwise the state of your health may
plummet."

"Are you threatening me?"

Jake gave him a bleak grin. "I am, yeah."

Knerr bent, brushing dust from his knee.
"Okay, sure, Cardigan, allright," he murmured
sullenly. "But, I better warn you, I'm going to
report this whole nasty incident to China Vargas."

"When you do, remind her not to put any
more nitwits dogging me."

Knerr took a deep breath, scowling at Jake.
Instead of saying anything, he pivoted on his
heel and went hurrying out of the alley.

Whistling a samba, Gomez strolled along the
Avenida Atlantica. On his right stretched the
bright midday ocean, on his left rose the multicolored towers of the Copacabana beachfront
buildings. In the palm trees that lined the

street, brightly plumed tropical birds fluttered, singing.

"Admirable workmanship," observed the curlyhaired private investigator, looking up at some of the robot birds.

Out over the Atlantic hovered a half dozen circular sunning platforms. As Gomez paused to watch, a deeply tanned and completely naked young woman stood up, moved gracefully to the edge of one of the platforms and then executed a flawless dive into the sea some forty feet below.

"Well, enough of tourist attractions," Gomez told himself. "Back to business."

He resumed his strolling and a block further along, just beyond a 2-story-high viewscreen showing General Silveira making a speech, he turned onto a mosaic pathway that led to a business tower.

The elevator greeted him warmly. "Glad to see you, *senhor*. What floor do you wish?"

"Fourteen."

"Are you certain?"

"Absolutely."

The elevator didn't move. From its wall-placed speaker it said, "The only thing located on fourteen is the Cafe Carioca, *senhor*. A low dive and, if you don't mind my saying so, a blotch on our otherwise pristine tenant list."

"Exactly," the detective agreed. "I have an appointment with an unsavory lout and, usu-

ally, unsavory louts prefer to hang out in low
dives. Upwards, if you please."

"As you wish, *senhor.*" Speaking no more,
the elevator carried him up to the floor he
wanted.

The Cafe Carioca lay behind an opaque plas-
tidoor. The door hissed open before Gomez
reached it. Beyond was a murky room dotted
with small tables. On an assortment of dangling perches sat a variety of mechanical par-
rots, and behind the small ebony bar glowed an
animated painting of a steamy stretch of Brazilian jungle.

There were less than ten patrons in the place
and one waiter. A robot dressed in the top half
of a tuxedo, the copperplated waiter came hurrying over to Gomez as the door shut him into
the cafe.

"A table, *senhor?*"

"No, I'm meeting . . . Ah, there he is over
yonder."

Following his gaze, the robot waiter inquired, "Are you a friend of Fado's?"

"Friend is probably too extravagant a word."
Gomez made his way to the small table where
the fat young informant was sitting.

Fado was in his late twenties, weighed just
under three hundred pounds and had a filigreed silver right arm encrusted with gems. He
was wearing a floral vidshirt and its bright
flowers flickered and changed patterns continually. *"Bom dia,* Gomez," he said.

Gomez sat opposite him. "You've upgraded your arm since last we met."

"That was, afterall, nearly two years ago." Spelled out on the metal arm was the word *Mãe*. Each letter was studded with a blend of diamonds and rubies. *"Mãe* is Portuguese for mother. I'm very fond of my—"

"I know. And how is the dear lady?"

"A pain in the ass, frankly. But as you may have noticed in life, Gomez, it's possible to be fond of someone who's a constant source of irritation."

Nodding, Gomez asked, "What have you found out for me?"

Pushing aside the glass of cupuassu punch he'd been sipping, Fado rested his arm atop the table. It had a computer terminal built into it. "Since I got your call, I've been actively tapping into my multitude of info sources."

"What do you have on Will Sparey?"

"Nada," he said apologetically. "Well, not exactly nothing, but not anything near something."

"Clarify that."

"The consensus thus far is that Will Sparey of the *GLA Fax-Times* was slaughtered by guerrillas during the final days of the final Brazil War," he said. "That was over a decade ago and it happened, far as anyone knows, somewhere in Mato Grosso."

"None of your sources thinks the guy's still alive somewhere?"

"No, but I'm putting ~~extra people to work~~ on dredging up info. That's going, by the way, to cost you an additional $1000."

Gomez, tapping his forefinger on the table, watched the nearest mechanical parrot. "Okay. Now what about Jean Marie Sparey?"

"She's a longtime Tekhead."

"What else?"

"She's twenty one, has resided in Brazil off and on for the past five years or so."

"Employed?"

"Not at the moment." Fado played with the keyboard on his arm. "Her last job was nearly a year ago, in Recife. She worked six months for an outfit called Comida, International."

"Which is a subsidiary of?"

Fado consulted his arm. "BenSan Industries."

"Once owned, no doubt, by the late Bennett Sands."

"That's him, *sim*. Didn't you and your hot-headed partner have a run-in with Sands recently?"

"We did," answered Gomez. "But Sands is currently among the angels and, far as I know, we don't have to worry about him."

"If you'd like I can . . . Hold it." Fado's filigreed arm had commenced making a faint beeping sound. "Message coming in." He depressed a key.

"I'll be taking my leave, Fado."

"Wait, this is for you, Gomez."

"Oh, so?"

Fado tapped the screen. "Do you know a lady named Alma Zingara?"

"Nope. Should I?"

"She's the editor of a weekly faxpaper called *Verdade*. That means truth in—"

"I know. Move on to the kernel of this."

"She found out somehow that you were asking about Sparey and, according to my contact, she's anxious to talk to you."

"Where and when?"

"Soon as you can get to her office. She's over Botafogo way." Fado gave him the address.

Pushing back his chair, Gomez rose. "Keep nosing around. I'll check back later."

"You, by the way, owe me $1500 for what I've already done."

"Put it on the tab." Smiling, Gomez took his leave.

= 8 =

THE DIMLIT ROOM in the private hospital was small and edged with shadows. It smelled of medicines and sickness. Over the humming, whirring and ticking of the life support machines surrounding the bed Jake could hear the sound of the slow, labored breathing of Jean Marie Sparey.

Standing near the bed, between the scanner that was providing continuous monitor pictures of the dying young woman's heart and a three-legged respirator, was a blackrobed robopriest. Ebony beads dangled from his metallic right hand and he was, very softly, reciting prayers for the repose of her soul.

The priest turned as Jake approached the bed. "It would be best, *senhor,*" he suggested quietly, "to leave her alone."

"She wants to talk to me. I'm Jake Cardigan."

"But the poor child is at death's—"

"Take a hike, Father Ambrose," suggested Jean Marie in her thin, dry voice.

She, slowly and with considerable effort, moved her right hand to touch the control panel on her bedframe. The bed whirred, raising her to a sitting position.

"My dear, you ought to be concentrating on *Deus* and not on—"

"Go away," she said, "please."

"Yeah, do that," Jake seconded. He took hold of the robot cleric's blackclad arm and gave him a start toward the doorway.

"Very well, little one. But I shall call on you again—if there's time."

"What a schmuck," observed Jean Marie. "Uncle Jake . . . I'm glad . . . you came."

He took hold of her frail hand, which was cold and damp. "I won't bother to ask how you're doing."

"I've been . . . seriously hooked on . . . Tek for . . . for much too long," she told him. "You know . . . how that can be."

Nodding, he asked, "What about your father?"

"I thought . . . he was . . . dead . . . one reason why I . . . got so serious about using . . . Tek, I guess."

"Will's not dead?"

"I've been living . . . in Rio again for about a

year . . . I keep coming back to Brazil . . . hoping
I'd . . . hear something about him."

"And have you?"

"Yes, Uncle Jake . . . and it's good news
. . . sort of . . . they told me that my father
. . . is alive . . . but he's . . . in serious trouble."

"What sort of trouble?"

"Not sure . . . but it's the kind . . . that can kill
you."

"Do you know where he is?"

"Only that he's . . . in Brazil . . . someplace
. . . but . . . he's going to need help to . . . get from
wherever he is . . . to here . . . I really do . . . want
to see him . . . once more."

"Who told you about him?"

"Couple of men contacted me . . . I think
they're tied in with . . . the Bulcão Tek cartel
. . . that's a major one down here . . . they said
. . . my dad wanted to see me . . . but couldn't
risk coming here . . . he needs help."

"When was this?"

"Hard to keep track of time lately . . . about
three weeks ago I think . . . I was still up and
around then . . . but I had another bad seizure
right after . . . ended up here . . . can you help,
Uncle Jake?"

"Sure," he promised. "How can I contact
these guys?"

"You have to contact . . . a man named Sargento."

"Know where I can find him?"

"No, but . . . people in Rio . . . they know how."

"Okay, we'll track him down."

"Who's . . . with you?"

"Sid Gomez."

"I remember him . . . curly haired and cute?"

"That pretty much sums up Gomez, yeah."

"Uncle Jake, I think I better . . . rest now . . . don't want to . . . but . . ." She drifted off into sleep.

Her thin hand gradually went slack in his. Jake let go, but remained watching the sleeping girl until an android doctor came into the shadowy room to remind him it was time to leave.

The plump, dark woman told Gomez, "Don't jiggle so much, okay?"

"Everywhere I go lately," complained the detective, "people question my identity."

Alma Zingara looked from him to the bank of viewscreens on the wall of her small, gadget-packed office. "Just want to compare you with what I have on Sid Gomez in my files," she said, studying the pictures and data that were showing on the various screens. "You seem to be who you say you are. Though you're not aging well."

"Most of those pics were taken within the past year, *chiquita*."

Shaking her head sympathetically, the editor said, "Well, yours is a stressful profession."

He leaned forward. "Now can we get to what you want to talk to me about?"

"I heard that you were asking about Will Sparey."

"True."

"Why?"

Gomez glanced toward the office's single window. Thick tangles of greenery masked any view. "It has to do with a current investigation by the Cosmos Detective Agency."

"I get the impression you think he's alive."

"We're looking into the possibility that he's alive."

Alma Zingara exhaled slowly, eyeing him. "You aren't telling me much, Gomez."

"I'm not," he agreed, starting to get up. "But then, I didn't send for you, you sent for me. If you're only after fodder for your paper, then—"

"I knew Will Sparey," she said, waving him back into the chair. "During the last war I worked with him."

"Oh, so?"

"We were pretty close," she continued. "So I was aware of what Will was really up to."

"You mean the lad was doing something besides covering the conflict for the *GLA Fax-Times?*"

She answered, "Will was . . . How'd you get in here?"

The door of her private office had come whispering open. A smiling chromeplated robot stepped over the threshold. He held a large bouquet of yellow roses in his metal left hand and had the word *Flores* etched across his wide silvery chest. *"Boa tarde,"* the robot said. "I'm here to deliver your birthday bouquet, *senhora."*

"Nobody can get through that door unless I release the lock from here," she said, slowly standing. "And this isn't my birthday."

"You're right, it's not," agreed the smiling robot. With his glittering right hand he yanked a lazgun out from among the roses.

—=9=—

"GET DOWN!" ORDERED Gomez, reaching for the stungun in his shoulder holster.

Alma Zingara started to duck down behind her metal desk.

The robot, tossing the bouquet of yellow roses aside, fired his lazgun at her.

Gomez shot at the mechanical man with his stungun.

The beam from the robot's weapon struck the editor before she had time to drop down behind her desk.

It sliced clean through her chest, cutting her body completely in two. Blood went splashing up against the viewscreens where Gomez's images had been.

When the stunbeam touched the robot, he

stiffened, rose up on tiptoe. His jaw dropped open, then clanked shut.

He let go his lazgun, swayed, thunked to his knees. He teetered, making a raspy gagging sound before falling forward. He hit the floor hard, crushing the fallen flowers beneath him.

Gomez, keeping his stungun in his hand, moved carefully to the doorway. The outer office was empty, the street beyond was sunny and quiet.

"Damn it," he muttered.

Walking back toward Alma Zingara's desk, he edged around and squeezed into the vidphone alcove next to it. Sitting down, he punched out the number of the Rio City Police.

There was blood splashed across the phone-screen.

Jake hadn't bothered activating the lights in the living room of their hotel suite. He was sitting in the twilight room, looking up at the ceiling, when his partner returned.

"I hope," said Gomez, touching the control panel and lighting up the room, "that you had a jollier afternoon than I did."

Jake eased up out of the armchair. "We can compare notes, but I doubt it."

"Did you spend an hour and thirty six minutes being queried by the Rio City Police?"

"Nope."

"*Bueno,* then I had the worst time."

"What were the cops asking you about?"

Sitting on the edge of the sofa, Gomez said, "First tell me about your meeting with Jean Marie."

"It was rough seeing her so close to dying." He shook his head. "She says some fellows in the Tek trade contacted her about three weeks back. They claim her father's alive, hiding out somewhere in Brazil. He'd like to see her but it's apparently dangerous for him to come out in the open."

"What's the *hombre* afraid of?"

"She doesn't know."

"How does Tek figure in this?"

"Could be Sparey's doing some kind of exposé of one of the big cartels."

"C'mon, that wouldn't explain where he's been all this time."

"No, it wouldn't. It's much more likely that he's working for the Tek dealers. Jean Marie, though, doesn't have any details."

Gomez scratched his head. "There's a hell of a lot going on, *amigo,* that we don't know anything about."

"That's my impression, too. Now explain why you spent the afternoon with the police."

"Well, whilst I was inquiring of one of my local informants for news of the present whereabouts of Will Sparey, word reached me that a lady name of Alma Zingara was most eager to chat with me," said Gomez. "The lady edits— make that edited—a liberal weekly news-sheet."

"She's dead?"

"As of this afternoon, *sí.*" Gomez went on to tell him what had happened at the editor's office.

When he concluded, Jake said, "Too bad she didn't get to tell you much."

"That's probably why they knocked her off— to keep her from passing on what she knew about Sparey."

"You think she knew where he is?"

"She was at least aware of what he was up to during the war. I'm not sure how any of that ties in with our present quest."

"What do the city cops think?"

"That she had a lot of enemies because of her frequent criticisms of the regime of the illustrious General Silveira."

"Her killing has to tie in with Sparey."

"I never got around to mentioning Sparey to them." Gomez wandered over to the window. "What's our next step?"

"Jean Marie gave me the name of a guy to talk to. His name is Sargento."

Gomez made a snorting noise. "Sargento, huh?"

"Know him?"

"Heard of him," said Gomez. "As I understand, it would take a massive public relations campaign to upgrade his image to that of weasel."

═ 10 ═

THE FAT WOMAN with the crinkly rainbow hair
lit a tobacco cigarette, coughed violently,
laughed, blinked her purple-shaded eyelids several times and said, "You're talking like a man
with a paper asshole, Gomez honey."

Gomez was perched on the edge of the fat
woman's lucite reception desk. Leaning closer
to her, he said, "$500 is a handsome fee, Mrs.
Cardwell."

She looked hopefully toward Jake, who was
sitting in a wicker chair across the DataDoll
showroom. "Sweetheart, tell this cheapskate I
can't give valuable information away for nothing."

Jake grinned. "Myself, I wouldn't pay more
than $400 for Sargento's present location."

Mrs. Cardwell paused to cough violently. "A couple of skinflints, that's what I'm locked in combat with," she complained, rolling her eyes and exhaling smoke.

Dropping free of her desk, Gomez strolled over to the nearest display pedestal. It held a deactivated android, a lovely blonde young woman, deeply tanned and entirely naked. "According to your DataDoll catalogue, I could enjoy a night on the town with this one for only $300."

"That's our loss leader this week. The other bimbos cost $1000 and up."

"Still, Mrs. Cardwell, feasting our eyes on Sargento isn't worth $200 more than an evening with a lovely andy."

"You're drawing a false parallel, honey. Boffing one of these bimbos isn't the same as getting information that's vital to the success of your current investigation." The fat woman, after coughing violently, nodded in Jake's direction. "Selling information is my sideline. It has different standards, and different fees, than the mechanized escort service. Tell Gomez that, Cardigan."

Jake got up. "We better go see your next contact, Sid."

Gomez was slowly circling a pedestal that held a black teenage girl in pink pajamas. "$550 is my final offer."

Mrs. Cardwell took a slow thoughtful drag of her bootleg cigarette, then sighed out smoke.

"You're meaner than a jaguar with the pip," she told him sourly. "But, okay." Hunching forward, she ran pudgy beringed fingers over her desk keyboard.

From out the printer that sat between two of the naked female androids ticked a sheet of yellow paper.

Gomez took it. "So Sargento's at the Casa Florenza boarding house over on Guanabara Bay?"

"That's what I wrote, isn't it? Now slip me the dough."

Folding the paper away into his trouser pocket, Gomez returned to her desk. "Here you have $200, Mrs. Cardwell. If Sargento is indeed where you say, the remainder will—"

"Wait now, honey. The paltry $550 fee is simply for providing you with an address, not for a guarantee that that rodent is still—"

"We'll see you anon," promised Gomez.

He and Jake headed out into the night.

Jake, since he stepped clear of the skycar first, encountered the man with the lazgun first.

The man was big, wide and bearded and he gripped the black weapon in his gloved left hand. He was standing in front of the high, thick hedge that separated the rutted lot from the ramshackle Casa Florenza boarding house. Nearby was a scraggly palm tree.

"Boa noite, senhor," he said quietly. "Climb back into your car, *se faz favor,* and fly away."

"Oh, sure, certainly," said Jake, grinning amiably. "We sure don't want to upset you or get in your way." He turned back toward the skycar.

Then he suddenly dropped to the ground, rolled rapidly to his left and tugged out his stungun.

He twisted, sat up and fired at the big man before he could get his lazgun aimed.

The beam of Jake's stungun hit the man in the belly. He went hopping back, arms flapping, until he collided with the trunk of the tree. His gun fell to the ground and he followed it.

Gomez, who'd drawn his own stungun, was looking carefully around. "Any idea what's afoot, *amigo?*"

Kneeling, Jake picked up the unconscious man's lazgun. "Possibly somebody doesn't want us to call on Sargento."

There was a warm wind drifting in across the dark waters of the bay. The high hedge and the fronds of the palm tree rattled quietly.

Jake moved closer to his partner. "We'd better approach the boarding house with—"

"Okay, Sargento, you miserable weasel," boomed an unseen amplified voice from out in front of the place. "We know you're cowering in there!"

"Have we chanced upon a police raid?" wondered Gomez.

Jake poked the fallen gunman with his boot. "This lunk is no cop."

"We'll give you five minutes to come out, Sargento. With Aunt Amalia's money."

Gomez observed, "Sounds like some past crime of Sargento's has caught up with him."

"This is Manuel Betancourt," continued the amplified voice. "I'm stationed by the front porch, thoroughly armed. My brother Jose is watching the back way and Jaime is standing guard over in the landing lot. Five minutes and then we come in and teach you a lesson."

"This may be the sort of lesson," said Gomez, "that will leave Sargento incapable of telling us much."

"Go around front and distract Manuel," suggested Jake. "I'll handle Jose and then we'll get Sargento out of here."

Gomez put his gun away and slipped unobtrusively through a break in the thick hedge.

Jake, holstering his stungun, walked across the lot and pushed through the hedge. He emerged about fifty yards from the rear of the rickety 3-story boarding house.

Crouched near the back entrance, intently watching the house and illuminated by the lightball that was floating over the doorway, was another large, moustached man. He had a lazrifle cradled against his broad chest.

Jake walked up to within ten feet of him. "Excuse me."

The man spun, pointing his rifle at Jake.

"Didn't mean to scare you," apologized Jake. "But I noticed there's a fellow—looks something like you—sprawled out in the lot over there."

"My brother Jaime?"

"Don't know who he is, but he's out cold. If he is your brother, you probably ought to go take a look," said Jake, easing closer. "He's covered with blood."

"Blood?"

"My guess would be that somebody knifed him."

"Damn it. Sargento must've slipped by us." Lowering the rifle, he started running for the hedge.

Jake waited until the man was just beyond him, then yanked out his stungun and shot him.

After Jose fell over, Jake scooped up the lazrifle and tossed it in the direction of the shaggy brush.

After listening for a few seconds, he went cautiously into the boarding house.

Halfway along the dimlit first floor hall a lean woman in a floppy green robe popped out of a doorway to confront him. "If this doesn't stop I'm going to call the police," she warned.

"It's been my experience, ma'am, that people who live in establishments like this rarely do that."

"I happen to own this building. I'm no less than Florenza."

"All the more reason to avoid trouble with

the law," he pointed out. "Which room is Sargento in?"

"I don't know if I should tell you, *senhor*."

"I'm not here to trounce him," he said. "I want to get him away from the people who do."

"Will you take him far away from my boarding house?"

"Miles," promised Jake.

"He's in 3C."

The front door popped open at the other end of the hallway.

Gomez entered. "Is all well?"

"Yeah," answered Jake. "Let's go up and rescue Sargento."

— ≡ 11 ≡ —

"I'M SAFE HERE," said Sargento, who was huddled in the corner of the restaurant booth. "I can trust the staff."

"The staff of Colonel Kilgore's Tea Shoppe #463," noted Gomez, "consists of one tacky robot in a greasy polka dot apron."

"But I can trust Edna," said the small leathery man. "She won't sell me out like those bastards at the boarding house."

Jake asked him, "Where's Will Sparey?"

Lifting his wraparound dark glasses and squinting at Jake, Sargento said, "We don't need to rush."

"I want to find out as much as we can before the next wave of irate citizens descends on you."

"Oh, those rotten Betancourts are an exception," Sargento assured him. "I'm well liked around Rio. You can ask anybody."

"The two dozen people I have asked," put in Gomez, "all rank you as a topseeded lowlife."

"What do they know? Besides, that's not a sufficient sampling."

"Will Sparey," repeated Jake.

Removing his dark glasses, the small man asked, "What do you know about his alleged disappearance years ago, Cardigan?"

"Not much. The story at the time was that a band of guerrillas in a wild part of Mato Grosso killed him."

"That's all that was. A story." Setting his glasses aside, Sargento fished a vial of clear liquid from the breast pocket of his plaid jacket. "Eyedrops."

While Sargento was lubricating his eyes, Gomez suggested, "Suppose you tell us what really happened."

"That's exactly what I intend to do, Gomez. Edna, a pot of mint tea and the usual trimmings. Put it on this gent's bill. That's all right by you, isn't it, Cardigan?"

"Yeah," said Jake. "Now tell us something."

"The air in Rio really bothers my eyes." He slipped the vial away. "Sparey wasn't killed by anyone. He's still alive." From a side pocket he drew an electrocomb and flicked it on. "You see, while he was covering the last war, he met some people." Sargento began working on his hair with the humming comb.

"What people?"

"Chief among them was . . . Ah, thank you, Edna."

The robot waitress had lurched over to their booth and slammed a tray down in front of Sargento. "You're looking quite dapper tonight, Sarge," she observed in a rusty voice.

"You really think so? Does my hair look okay to you?"

"It looks right lovely."

"You see, Edna, I had an encounter earlier in the evening with some fellows who mussed me up."

"It doesn't show. You look absolutely—"

"That'll be all," Gomez told her.

"Very well, sir, I'm sure."

"Wait a minute, Edna. I want your opinion of my eyes."

"Soulful."

"They've been awfully bloodshot of late."

"Oh, they're bloodshot, Sarge, but that doesn't prevent them from still being very soulful. Not a bit, no," said the robot waitress. "Oh, and I'm sorry about the ruddy dust on the plum cake. It's the last blinking slice and, wouldn't you know, I went and dropped it a few times back in the blooming pantry."

"Don't worry, Edna."

Jake urged, "Get back to Sparey."

Sargento applied the electrocomb to the

greying hair at his left temple. "I've found that personal appearance is all important in this world. That and taking the time to be cordial to—"

"Apparently your good grooming didn't impress the Betancourts." Gomez reached across the table and took hold of the man's arm. "Concentrate on informing us about Sparey, Sarge."

"A little background is called for, Gomez. Which is what I've been attempting to provide you." He extricated his arm. "Sparey, you see, went to work for the biggest Tek cartel in these parts. It was run back then by a gentleman named Antonio Bulcão." He shut off his comb. "Sparey, so I've been told, had a lot of debts." He glanced over at Jake for confirmation.

Jake nodded. "He liked to gamble."

"That's why he went to work for Bulcão, using many of the contacts he had here in Brazil," said the small man. "He kept getting increasingly involved in the Tek trade, may even have helped kill a few of the cartel's rivals. Finally, so I've been told, he decided it would be much safer if the world thought he'd passed on."

"Why didn't he let his daughter know what he was going to do?"

"He thought it would be best if she really thought he was dead and gone. Sparey did, however, set up a trust fund for her, which was administered anonymously," continued Sargento. "He didn't anticipate, obviously, that the kid could get hooked on Tek herself or that she'd come down here to look for traces of him."

"She's been on Tek for years," mentioned Gomez. "How come Sparey is just now getting around to wanting to see her?"

"Hard to say. Maybe it's because he heard she was about to croak." He shrugged his narrow shoulders. "All I know for certain is that Sparey wants to quit the Tek trade, but is afraid that Bulcão's people won't let him. So he got word to Jean Marie and instructed her to contact Cardigan for him. See, Cardigan, he trusts you." Sargento pressed his palm against the side of the teapot. "He wants somebody to come get him and escort him safely to Rio. Then he plans to talk to the International Drug Control Agency, exchange what he knows for protection. He wants to see his daughter before she dies, too."

"She thinks the guys who contacted her are with the Bulcão outfit," said Jake. "How does that work?"

"No, they used to be, but not now. They're friends of Sparey, though, and they took a risk for him. Contacted Jean Marie, filled me in, then took off for elsewhere."

"This is just talk," Jake said. "So far."

The small man reached inside his plaid coat, producing a three dimensional photo. He handed it across. "Is that him?"

The picture showed a heavyset black man,

nearly bald, standing uneasily in a sunfilled jungle clearing.

Jake studied it for a moment. "It looks like Will."

"You'll notice he's no longer the thin youthful fellow he was back when he was a reporter. That indicates this is a recent pic."

Passing the picture to his partner, Jake said, "A photo can be faked."

"That's so, Cardigan." Shrugging, Sargento picked up the stained teapot. "Want any of this stuff?"

"Nope."

Pouring mint tea into a cracked cup, he said, "I have no idea, Cardigan. What I'm getting at is, I was slipped that pic and told to hand it over to you. They also briefed me on what to tell you. It could be authentic and true, it could be moonshine and bullshit. Take your pick."

"What's next?"

"You have to go to the city of Brasilia. Know where that is?"

"Sure. And?"

"Fellow calling himself Senhor Macaco will meet you there. Macaco is Portuguese for something or other."

"Monkey," supplied Gomez.

"Yeah, that's it. Anybody who nicknames himself after a monkey has pretty low self esteem in my book." He sipped his tea. "At any rate, he'll be there for the next two days." Taking back the picture, he scrawled an address across the back. "Go see him or not, it's up to you. I don't suppose you'd care for any of this plum cake either?"

—= 12 =—

THEIR SKYCAR HEADED inland through the hazy morning toward the Central Plateau region of Brazil.

Jake, after punching out the flight pattern on the control panel, had settled back in the pilot seat.

Gomez, who occupied the passenger seat, was sipping a cup of nearcaf. "You knew Will Sparey fairly well," he said finally. "A lot better than I did anyway."

"That's right, yeah."

"He strike you, back then, as the sort of guy who'd get involved in the Tek trade?"

"Hard to tell," said Jake. "I do know his gambling used to get him pretty deeply in debt."

"And you think that once he came down here

he got himself so seriously in hock that he let the Bulcão cartel boys recruit him?"

Jake looked over at his partner. "What's bothering you?"

"Well, as you know, I did some nosing around on my own," he answered. "Everybody I chatted with seems convinced that Sparey has been completely and totally defunct for many a moon."

"His daughter doesn't think so."

"The young lady is ailing. She wants to believe he's still extant."

"All we're going to do is determine if he's alive or not. And if he is, we'll help him get out safely."

"I know you used to bounce little Jean Marie on your knee in days gone by." Gomez refilled his cup from the dash nozzle. "But she did, keep in mind, once work for that old buddy of ours, Bennett Sands."

"Sands is dead."

"A large number of his former associates in the Tek business are still above the ground, though."

"I don't feel Jean Marie is conning me," Jake told him. "But even if she is, I still want to follow through on this."

"Oh, so?"

"If somebody is trying to decoy us, I'm interested in finding out exactly who they are," said Jake. "Find out and then incapacitate them."

"At which point they'll be less of a threat to our wellbeing."

"And less of a threat to Beth," added Jake.

A harsh wind was blowing across Brasilia as Jake guided their skycar down toward the city. A thick orange dust swirled through the weedy overgrown streets and brushed at the stark glass and metal buildings.

Below them in the swirling clouds of orange flashed a lightsign offering SAFE PARKING!

"Avoid that lot," advised Gomez. "My sources inform me that the one operated by Gonsalvez Enterprises is more reliable."

"There it is up ahead, beyond that dry lake."

The lightsigns on the Gonsalvez landing lot promised 99% SAFE! GUARDED BY GUNBOTS!

Just as Jake was about to tap out a landing pattern, a crimson skyvan came swooping down across their path.

Using the manual controls, Jake dived their skycar and avoided a collision.

As the crimson van sailed by close above them, it gave out a harsh hooting sound.

Gomez frowned up at it. "I suppose you can't expect careful, courteous flying from lads who have neon snakes and skulls decorating their vehicle."

"Ah, youth," said Jake.

As their skycar settled onto a rectangle of orange-brown ground, a voice came out of their dash speaker. "Remain inside your vehicle, *sen-*

hores, while we run through a quick routine check to determine if it's stolen, involved in a crime or otherwise undesirable. *Muito obrigado."*

"Have I mentioned," said Gomez, "that Brasilia has a reputation for being a seedy and wide open community?"

"Nope, but I figured that out on my own."

The office building across the way had most of its upper walls missing. Draped from two rusted girders was a globanner proclaiming CHEAPEST SEX IN TOWN! Next to it stood a gambling casino whose windows had long since been replaced with plastarps and large sheets of corrugated metal. In the dusty roadway alongside the landing lot two dozen or so citizens were watching a dogfight and betting on the outcome.

"Your car passes muster," announced the voice of the lot computer. "You can leave your seats and go on about your business. Be certain you pay in advance as you leave. Be certain also that you get your lot passes. Anyone without a pass will be shot if he or she attempts to enter this area."

"That makes me feel secure." Gomez got out, stretched.

A few yards away, next to a lemon yellow skycar, was stationed a large black-enameled guardbot with a lazgun built into his right hand. "Don't loiter."

"We don't intend to loiter in your lot," said Gomez, "nor in your fair city."

They were only a half block from the lot when the crimson skyvan dropped down to land in the dusty road ahead of them.

The door on the driveside popped open and a lean youth stumbled out. He wore glopants and an animated shirt that showed naked women dancing. Around his neck hung an electroknife on a golden chain. His shaved head was a mixture of tattooed snake designs and recent scabs.

"Hey, scum!" he yelled.

Gomez halted. "Could this lout be addressing us, do you think?"

Jake stopped. "That wouldn't be very smart of him."

Another door came flapping open and two more similar young men disembarked.

The largest said, "You assholes came near to hitting us just now, do you know?"

Jake grinned thinly. "Let me give you some helpful advice," he said. "Don't carry this any further."

"You trying to order us around?" inquired the one with the scabs, fingering his knife. "You nearly knocked us clean out of the sky and now—"

Gomez said, "Boys, before anything unpleasant occurs, vacate the area."

"We'll vacate your ass," threatened the largest. He had a metal right arm, which looked to have been borrowed from a chromeplated robot. Held in its silvery fingers was a dented black lazgun. "You came close to cracking us up. Can't you see what a nice van that is? You crack that up, you're in deep trouble."

"We're going to show you," said the lean one with scabs, "that you can't dick around with us."

Jake sighed. All at once his stungun was in his hand.

He fired at the young man with the metallic right arm.

The youth stiffened, eyes going wide. His fingers fanned out, the gun dropped into the orange dust.

Gomez's stungun was in his hand now. With the thumb of his other hand he pointed skyward. "Bon voyage," he said.

The one Jake had stunned toppled over. Dust huffed up all around him when he hit the ground.

The driver of the crimson van complained, "You nearly killed him."

"Nope, we never kill anybody the first time around," Gomez assured him. "It's only when they give evidence of not having learned their lesson that we resort to that."

The third young man spoke. "Let's go," he said, hurrying back inside the van.

"Well," said the other one as he let go of his

knife, "we'll forget about it this time. But, you know, try to drive carefully in the future."

Jake and Gomez kept their guns drawn until they were several blocks from the lot.

⎯ ⎯ 13 ⎯ ⎯

THERE WAS NO plastiglass in the windows of the office. The wind scattered orange dust across the cracked mosaic flooring, sprinkled it over the weather-stained lucite desk and the half dozen lopsided chairs.

Senhor Macaco explained, "This isn't my regular office."

"That's comforting to know." Gomez wiped gritty dust from his forehead with a plyochief. "We'd hate to think of you spending the rest of your natural life here."

Jake was straddling a wobbly chair near the desk, watching the wrinkled little man. "What can you tell us about the whereabouts of Will Sparey?"

Macaco plucked a banana from the green

bunch sitting atop the dusty desk. "I wish you to understand, *senhores,* that I'm nothing more than a go-between in this whole affair," he explained, starting to peel the banana. "Should there be any unfortunate repercussions, I want it definitely established that I am merely doing a job and am in no way a partisan."

Nodding, Jake said, "How do we get to Sparey?"

"Un momento." The small, whitesuited little man set the partially peeled banana aside. From an inside pocket of his wrinkled jacket he withdrew a plump packet of assorted papers and photos. Placing it on the desk, he unwound the plastrip holding the material together. "Everything in this world, *senhores,* is a matter of procedures and routines, I find."

"What's that got to do with—"

"Pacienca." Macaco slowly and carefully spread out the papers, hunching, squinting. "Ah, *sim."* Selecting a three dimensional photograph, he brought it up close to his cloudy eyes. "I have here a recent portrait of you two *cavalheiros."* After studying it and them, Macaco gave a satisfied tick of his head. "You appear to be who you claim."

Jake shifted in his chair. "How far is Sparey from here?"

"Keep in mind that I have never met the man." After carefully gathering up the papers and pictures, he fastened them up again. "I was instructed to pass along a map." He slipped the packet away and searched another pocket, producing a folded sheet of blue faxpaper. "This, *senhores,* is that very map."

Walking over, Gomez took it. "Can you explain this a bit?" he requested after unfolding it and studying it.

"Sim, of course."

Gomez spread the map out on the desk. "Where exactly is this Fazenda Cinca?"

Macaco stretched up out of his chair, frowning across at the map. "Forgive me, the coordinates have been left off." In another of his pockets he found an electropen. He wrote on the faxpaper. "There, that takes care of the problem. Fazenda Cinca, which means, by the way, Ranch Five in my language, lies approximately three hundred miles to the Southwest. Some fifty or so years ago the then Brazilian government began an ambitious reforestation project there, to replace jungle that had been destroyed by earlier slash-and-burn agricultural practices among the locals. The project failed many years since, but Fazenda Cinca is still there. It was once the base of operations for that area."

Jake asked, "Is Sparey holed up there?"

"Sim, with a few friends looking after him, trusted friends."

Gomez folded up the map. "Do Sparey and these trusted cronies know we're enroute?"

"Word has been sent." Macaco picked up the banana, taking a small bite. "I do believe, *sen-*

hores, that unless you have further enquiries, this ends our little get-together."

Jake stood. "Nope, that's all."

"Allow me to wish you a safe journey into the wilderness," called Senhor Macaco as they headed out the doorless doorway.

Beneath them stretched an endless green. As the day faded the multiple shades of green of the forest began to change, deepening and darkening.

Gomez was in the pilot seat, studying the tiny navigation screen on the dash. "We should be at Fazenda Cinca in another ten minutes," he said.

Jake had been absently watching the jungle unfurl thousands of feet below their skycar. "Let's fly over whatever buildings are still there a few times before setting down." He straightened up in his seat. "I want to get an idea of how many folks are awaiting us."

"This being a sophisticated vehicle, we can ascertain that from up here."

Nodding, Jake activated a scanner screen on the panel before him.

The craft began descending down through the darkening day. The sky was streaked with thin streamers of cloud.

"You can see the buildings now," said Gomez. "Up ahead on our left. Looks like the forest has taken some of them back."

In the growing dusk below sat three large

domed buildings. There had once been a clearing but that was thick with new growth, and numerous vines were crawling over the curved plastiglass roofs of the complex.

Gomez took back the control of their skycar and started flying it in a circling pattern 1500 feet over the area. "These old eyes don't spot any signs of a welcoming committee," he said after a moment. "What are our gadgets getting?"

Jake touched the keyboard that controlled the screen. "There's a faint indication of body heat," he said. "However . . ." He fingered the keys again. "Nope, it's nothing but small animals. No humans."

Dropping down a couple hundred feet lower, Gomez executed another slow circuit. "Not even one long lost reporter?"

"Not according to—"

A sudden strident beeping burst out of the speaker grid. At the same time Jake's screen started flashing an intense red.

"Something's down there," said Gomez, "that our secsystem isn't happy about."

Jake flipped on another screen. "It's located in the center building of the complex. But I can't get a reading on exactly what—"

"Madre!" exclaimed Gomez.

Their skycar died, ceased to function. It quivered, rattled, then nosed over and began to plummet earthward.

═14═

It was a grey misty morning in Berkeley and Beth Kittridge was scheduled to leave for Berlin in less than an hour.

She hadn't packed yet.

Once again she walked to the vidphone alcove. Sitting, she punched out the same number she'd tried six minutes earlier.

After three rings the robot receptionist appeared on the screen. "San Francisco Branch Office, International Drug Control Agency. Business hours haven't yet begun, but you . . . Oh, good morning again, Miss Kittridge."

"Is Director MacQuarrie there yet?"

"No, miss, he still hasn't arrived. And I haven't been able to locate him."

Hanging up, Beth tried a Greater LA number.

Dan Cardigan, still in his pajamas, answered on the second ring. "Morning, Beth. I was going to phone you."

"Have you heard from him?"

Shaking his head, Jake's son answered, "Nope. I was wondering if you had."

"Not a word," admitted Beth. "What I'm trying to do, Dan, is get the IDCA to let me postpone testifying for a few days. Then I can travel down to Rio and try to find out what's happened to Jake."

"You probably won't have to do that," said Dan. "More than likely he and Gomez are just someplace where they can't get to any—"

"It's been three days. They've got a communication unit in their skycar."

"Sure, but Sparey could be off in the jungle, somewhere that you can only reach on foot or—"

"They have belt-communicators, too."

"You can't always safely use those, though."

"Do you honestly believe nothing's happened to them?"

"I'm trying to," Dan answered. "Dad's told me that there are times in some investigations when you can't risk contacting—"

"He promised me he'd be here by today."

"I know, Beth. But he and Gomez are first rate operatives and—"

"Have you talked to Bascom today?"

"Not yet, he's never awake this early. But he phoned me last night."

"He phoned me, too. Gave me the usual pitch about the Cosmos Detective Agency putting the best men on this. He swore they'd find out why nobody's heard from Jake or Gomez for so long."

"Cosmos does have a lot of good investigators to—"

"Excuse me, Dan. Someone's at the door. Call me soon as you hear anything."

Agent Neal was on her doorstep. He looked both weary and unhappy. "You about ready to go, Beth? We have to start for—"

"I'm not going," she told him. "Not until I hear something definite about Jake Cardigan."

Neal shook his head. "Director MacQuarrie's been in touch with us."

"He has? I've been trying to reach him for—"

"Director MacQuarrie wants me to convey his concern over Jake," continued Agent Neal. "But we have to depart for Berlin as planned."

"Emmett, there must be—"

"If you don't agree to come along voluntarily, I'm instructed to take you into custody and escort you to Berlin." He didn't meet her eyes.

"Staying here is more important to me."

"I know, Beth, but we're under orders."

"Maybe if I can talk to MacQuarrie directly."

"You won't be able to do that."

After a few seconds she said, "All right. I'll go along with you."

"I'll help you pack," the agent offered.

* * *

By cutting his last class at the academy, Dan was able to get to the Cosmos offices by a few minutes after three that afternoon.

Walt Bascom looked up from the scatter of files spread across his desk as the young man came striding in. "Did we have an appointment, Danny?"

"No, and don't call me Danny."

"Dan, why have you barged into my private—"

"I got the feeling you haven't been telling me everything you know about my father. You're holding back with me—and with Beth Kittridge."

"I hear she's enroute to Berlin."

"She left this morning, yeah." Dan walked up close to the agency chief. "You know my dad was planning to go with her. It would take something damn serious to—"

"Sit down, Dan."

Dan sat on the edge of a chair facing the desk. "Is he dead?"

"I have no idea what shape he and Gomez are in," Bascom answered. "We know they took off for Brasilia three days ago." He spread his hands wide. "That's the last anybody's heard."

"But what are you doing about—"

"I already told you that I've sent ops to Rio to find out what happened."

"But they haven't, have they, learned a damn thing?"

"Not thus far," admitted Bascom.

"That girl—Jean Marie Sparey. Doesn't she know anything?"

Sitting back, Bascom steepled his stubby fingers. "I'm inclined to think she does," he said. "The only trouble is—we can't find the little lady."

"But she's in that damn hospital—dying."

"So we thought. In fact, I shed several sincere tears over the sad vidtape she sent along."

"Where is she?"

"Not in the São Jose Private Hospital in Rio de Janeiro," answered the agency head. "Jean Marie isn't there anymore—nor are the three medics, one human and two andies, who were allegedly looking after her. The hospital officials claim they have no notion of where they all went. Miss Sparey and crew were last seen on the morning of the day your dad and Gomez left Rio."

"Then she must've been faking. She set my father and Gomez up."

"It could mean that, it could mean that she was kidnapped to keep her from talking to us," he said. "My ops have also found out, which does little to cheer me, that most of the other people whom Jake and Gomez talked to down there are also among the missing."

"Damn it." Dan got to his feet. "This whole case was just some kind of dodge. A plan to kill them."

"Maybe."

"Maybe? Good Christ, you know damn well that—"

"Easy, Dan. All I know for sure is that neither your dad nor Gomez has reported in for three days," Bascom said. "We don't have enough facts yet to speculate much."

"There's got to be something more we can do. Do right now."

"Jake is a good man, so is Gomez. I'm still inclined to bet that if they're in a mess, they can get themselves out," the agency chief said. "You better head for home now. I'll contact you soon as any news comes in."

Dan stood, hesitant, for a moment. "Okay," he said finally, turning away and leaving the office.

— ≡ 15 ≡ —

JAKE WAS WAITING for Beth in Berlin.

It was on the morning after she arrived in the
city that they met. A cold grey morning filled
with heavy rain.

Beth, accompanied by Agents Neal and
Griggs, had just stepped free of an IDCA land-
car near the side entrance to the World Drug
Court on Potsdamerplatz.

There were ten armed guards, human and
robot, lining each side of the long passway from
the curb to the narrow entry gate. All around
them, huddling under dark umbrellas, a small
crowd of curious onlookers had gathered.

Beth was only a few steps from the car when
she saw Jake.

He was pushing his way through the bystanders, waving, trying to attract her attention. "Beth!" he called, grinning his familiar grin. "Thought for awhile I wasn't going to make it."

"Jake!" Her smile turned into a pleased laugh. She pulled free of the grip of Agent Griggs, ran the fifteen feet to where he stood. "My god, what happened to you?"

"Long story."

A uniformed Berlin policeman was standing between Jake and the young woman, warning him back with his drawn stungun.

"It's all right, officer," she said. "He's okay. I know him. Please, stand aside."

"I'm sorry, Miss Kittridge." He held out his free hand and gently pushed her back.

"Jake, I was so damned worried," she said around the cop. "Where were you?"

"Gomez and I ran into some extra trouble. Tell you about it later. You okay?"

"I'm fine—now." Using her elbow, she started to nudge the officer out of the way.

"Beth, wait a minute." Agent Neal had come trotting over. He reached out to grab her.

"Oh, really, Emmett." She eluded him, pushed around the policeman. She put her arms around Jake. "I'm so glad—"

There was an enormous explosion.

─═ 16 ═──

IT WAS A small town on the edge of the vast forest. Just a scatter of low buildings and a couple of streets sitting there in the bright morning sunlight.

Jake spotted the cafe first. "They ought to have a vidphone there," he said, leaving the jungle trail and starting for it.

Gomez, limping some, followed Jake onto the dusty street. "I'm hoping they can also provide food and beverages," he said. "After living off the land for several days, I'm ready for—"

"Beth must be in Berlin by now," said Jake, hurrying, his footfalls stirring up dust. "I'll have to contact the IDCA office there to find out where she's staying."

"If we call Cosmos first, Bascom will know what—"

"Rather do it my way, Sid."

The cafe had a rickety verandah running along its front. The name of the place, judging by the single word scrawled on the window in milky paint, was LIMAO'S.

Jake went running up the shaky wooden steps, pushed through the lopsided swing doors.

There were only three people in the dining room, plus a sleeping dog and a very old parrot.

The two customers were at separate tables and the waiter, a gaunt man in white trousers and a tattered polka dot shirt, was leaning against a crooked wooden pillar. They were all watching a dirt-smeared vidwall screen.

Jake was about to ask where the phone was, when Beth appeared on the screen.

It was footage taken a few months earlier at a conference in San Francisco. She was smiling, making her way into a meeting hall, politely refusing to answer any questions about the Kittridge anti-Tek system.

A newsman, speaking Portuguese, started to explain.

Jake couldn't make out every word, but he got most of them.

". . . Beth Kittridge was twenty seven when she . . . death . . . this morning . . . in Berlin . . ."

Everything around him seemed to fade away, to vanish from the room. There was only Jake, feeling suddenly very cold, and the images on the wall.

As he watched, the wall showed him Beth getting out of a landcar in Berlin that morning. Agent Neal was with her and Agent Griggs.

Jake seemed to be there, too. At the edge of the small surrounding crowd, working his way closer to Beth.

He sensed what was going to happen. "No—it's a kamikaze!" he warned.

But Beth didn't pay any attention to him. She shook free of Griggs. She dodged Neal. She pushed by the German cop.

"No!" shouted Jake.

She put her arms around the other Jake, started to kiss him.

Then came the explosion and she . . .

Jake turned away. He couldn't watch that.

"That's a damn shame," observed the gaunt waiter.

"And what a waste," chuckled a fat man who was having sausage for breakfast. "A nice piece like that."

Jake went charging over to him. He grabbed the fat man's shirt front, jerked him out of his chair.

He didn't say anything, simply started punching the man in the face as hard as he could.

Gomez got hold of him in a bear hug from behind. "Jake, c'mon! Leave the guy alone."

"Bastard." Jake tried to keep hitting at the fat bloody face.

Tugging harder, his partner dragged him clear. "Not his fault."

Jake tore free of Gomez, staggered, stumbled. He sat down in a wooden chair. "They killed her," he said slowly. "Bastards killed Beth."

"Yeah."

Jake leaned far forward, put his hands out flat on his knees. Very quietly he started to sob. "That's what this was all about," he said in a voice that was not quite his.

⹀⹀ 17 ⹀⹀

THE RIO HOTEL room started talking to Gomez
at a few minutes before 8 A.M. the next morning.

"Bom dia, senhor," said the wallspeaker near
the head of his floating bed. "There is a visitor
in the lobby who desires to come up to your
suite."

Blinking a few times, yawning once, Gomez
elbowed himself into a sitting position. "Oh,
so?" he managed to say.

"Sim. His name is Dan Cardigan."

"Oh, then you don't want me. Contact Jake
Cardigan in the other bedroom." He started to
stretch out again.

"We've already tried Senhor Cardigan's
room. There was no answer. Do you wish us to
detain the young man down here until—"

"That's okay, send the lad on up." Sitting on the edge of the bed, Gomez rubbed his eyes, tried a few yawns and then, reluctantly, left the wide oval bed.

He and Jake had been out until near 3 A.M., asking questions all over Rio, trying to get a lead on the present whereabouts of Jean Marie Sparey. They'd had no luck whatsoever, even with the other Cosmos operatives Bascom had sent down helping them.

He located his clothes where he'd discarded them a few hours earlier. When the door announced a visitor, Gomez was dressed and nearly wide awake.

"Good morning, *amigo,*" he said, letting Dan in.

"Don't lecture me about coming here," requested the young man. "I got a special leave from the academy, so I'm not in trouble. When I talked to my dad on the phone yesterday afternoon— Well, I thought he might need me down here."

"Good idea." Gomez led him into the living room.

Glancing around, Dan asked, "Where is he?"

Gomez crossed to the door of Jake's room and knocked. He waited a half a minute before opening the door. "The answer to your inquiry, Daniel, is somewhere other than here."

Hurrying over, Dan looked into the empty room. "He didn't even sleep in the bed."

"He must've sneaked away after I turned in."

"Where to?"

Shrugging, Gomez turned away. "Probably wanted to follow up on something."

Dan caught his arm. "That's not what you really think, is it, Sid?"

Facing him, Gomez attempted to look guileless. "Eh?"

"You figure he's probably off at some damn Tek house. The shock of Beth's death has—"

"I don't figure anything, lad." He nodded toward a sofa. "Sit yourself down."

"Don't feel like sitting. He blames himself for her death, doesn't he?"

Gomez nodded. "That he does, *sí*."

"But he couldn't have known that—"

"He thinks he should've tumbled earlier that this was just a flimflam to get him out of the way."

"But why would they go through all this trouble? What I mean is, if they didn't want him to be around to protect Beth—why not just try to kill him?"

Shaking his head, Gomez said, "We're not talking about efficiency and logic here, my boy. These guys, whoever worked this one out, wanted to kill Beth, sure. But they also wanted to *hurt* Jake. See, revenge is sometimes much more fun if your victim is around to suffer."

"You're saying they didn't want to kill him?"

"Exactly, Daniel. Because they know blaming himself for her death is going to hurt him one hell of a lot."

"They really must hate him."

"That they do. They wanted Beth out of the way, but this was also an act of vengeance against Jake."

Dan walked over to the blanked windows. "He didn't tell me much on the phone," he said. "What exactly happened to you guys after Brasilia?"

"When we got way out in the wilds, to a place known as Fazenda Cinca, we encountered a powerful disabling generator. They'd set it up in one of the old buildings. Soon as we flew within range, the damn thing killed our skycar. Knocked out the engine, the communication system, even the nearcaf machine. It cooked our pocketphones, too. Jake managed to crash land safely, but we were completely stranded and cut off in the middle of the woods."

"So you did what?"

"Hiked back to civilization—or to a near approximation thereof," answered the detective. "We lived off the supplies we salvaged from our skycar. When those ran out, we dined on woodland produce and game. That was a challenge, too, since even our stunguns had been rendered defunct."

"Well, all right," said Dan, nodding. "Now we have to go out and find my father."

"No, we have to order breakfast first."

"I'm not up to—"

"I am, however," Gomez assured him. "After that, you'll remain here watching the vidwall or playing with the viewindow. I'll go out and—"

"But something could happen to him while you're dawdling."

"They're not going to kill him, Dan. Not for awhile. They're still enjoying watching him suffer."

He walked over to the vidphone and buzzed room service.

Beth wasn't dead.

When Jake reached the cottage high in the Berkeley hills, she was there.

None of the IDCA agents was around, though. The security robot wasn't at his post either.

That bothered Jake and before taking Beth in his arms he asked, "How come no guards? That's not smart."

She laughed, slipping her arms around him and kissing him on the cheek. "The Teklords think I'm dead."

"Sure, but even so—"

"Relax, darling. You really worry too much."

"After what happened in Berlin, I—"

"But that wasn't me, Jake. It was just an android dupe," Beth explained, hugging him.

"What about Agent Neal? He was killed, too."

"Another andy."

"You should've told me what you were planning."

"I tried, but couldn't reach you."

"My fault there, yeah. I let them sucker me out into the middle of nowhere."

"But it's all right, Jake. There was no real harm done."

Jake held her tightly, aware of the warmth of her. "When I saw you die, it was like—"

"I didn't die, darling. I'm right here." She kissed him.

After a moment he said, "You know, Beth, there are a lot of things I never got around to telling you. About how much I love you, how much you've changed my life."

"I'm aware of all that," she assured him, laughing gently. "There are better ways than words for expressing feelings like those."

"Sometimes, though, it's important to say things right out," he said. "From here on I'm going to try."

"I'm quite content with you the way you are."

"Well, maybe I'm not. So humor me, huh?"

She smiled. "Okay." She stepped back from him, then reached out to take hold of his right hand in both of hers. "I'll be forthright with you right now—let's go into the bedroom."

"That's a good idea."

But there was someone in the bed.

She sat up, giggling, when Jake crossed the threshold. "Hi, Uncle Jake."

Jake, angry, pulled away from Beth to go

walking over to Jean Marie Sparey. "What are you doing here?"

"Beth and I are old friends. Didn't she tell you?"

He turned to Beth. "This girl set me up."

"No, I didn't, Uncle Jake. Get in bed now and we'll explain everything. Won't we, Beth?"

Jake shook his head. "This isn't what I ordered. Jean Marie isn't supposed to be here at all."

Beth came over, smiling, and mussed his hair. "Don't pout, Jake. It makes you look so old."

"Everything is wrong. I'm supposed to be in control."

"Shit," said Jean Marie, "you don't control a damn thing anymore, Uncle Jake."

"That's right," seconded Beth. "Not even your Tek dreams, dear."

"No!" shouted Jake at the two women. "You're not—"

"Welcome back, *amigo.*"

Jake blinked, took a gasping breath. He was back in the dimlit private cubicle of the Tek joint. Sitting in the ancient fat armchair again, hooked up to a Brainbox.

"You're a pretty good detective," he told his partner.

"You weren't that hard to find." Gomez was leaning against a dirty pink wall.

"Sermon coming?"

"Nope. Soon as you're through feeling sorry

for yourself, though, we can head back for the hotel," he said. "Dan's there."

"How the hell did he—"

"He was concerned about you," Gomez told him. "Kid got the notion you might crack under the stress and do something dumb. Dan arranged a special leave and hopped down here."

"I'm not back on Tek, Sid."

"Sure, *sí*. And this isn't even a Tek parlor and that's not a Brainbox you've got your *cabeza* hooked up to."

Jake yanked the electrodes off his head. "I mean this was just a one-shot thing."

His partner said, "That makes, I think, the third time you've told me that lately."

"God damn it! She's dead!" Jake got up, swaying, clenching his fists.

"That's absolutely true, *amigo*. And Beth is just as dead now as she was before you started frying your fucking brains with that stuff."

"You don't know what I was going through," Jake told him. "Nobody does."

"That's right, sure, because you're the only *hombre* on Earth who ever lost someone before he was ready for it," said Gomez. "C'mon, *amigo*, and wake up. That's what being alive is about, learning how to lose things you think you can't live without."

"Didn't you promise no sermons?"

"This ain't a sermon. It's a lecture—and I'm getting as tired of it as you must be."

Jake sighed out a breath. "Okay, okay," he

said. "I tend to fall back on Tek when things get too rough. Does Dan know where I am?"

"He's got a pretty fair idea."

"I'll tell him what I did," decided Jake. "No use lying."

"Especially about the obvious."

"I guess it is pretty obvious, huh?"

"Yep."

"Worst part is—the damn Tek didn't even help any. I wanted a simple, comforting illusion. One where Beth is still alive." He moved, feet a little clumsy, toward the doorway. "What I got was a nightmare."

"Defective chip maybe."

"No, it's me. My brain won't let me bullshit it anymore."

Gomez asked, "You about through wallowing in grief, *amigo?*"

"Probably. Why?"

"Got a call from Bascom just before I left to beat the bush for you," replied his partner. "Cosmos has been retained to look into the killings in Berlin."

"Representing what client?"

"Bascom won't say, but he implied it's a government agency. One that suspects the murders don't smell quite right."

"I don't think we can find out anything more here in Brazil," Jake said. "I was planning to head for Germany on my own anyway."

"Are you up to taking on this job?"

"I am, Sid, don't worry. I won't fall back on Tek again."

"There's nothing wrong, you know, with getting hit hard by something. The thing is, when you—"

"I won't screw up again," he promised. "Now I want to see Dan and then get him sent back home safely. When do we leave for Germany?"

"Five P.M.," answered Gomez.

— ≡ 18 ≡ —

THE TUBE TRAIN slid to a stop at the skyport platform.

"This is the Europe Wing, ladies and gentlemen," announced the overhead speakers in their car. The message was delivered first in Portuguese, then in English.

Jake and Gomez gathered their luggage from the racks, with Dan helping, and moved to the nearest exit from the car.

The doors remained shut.

Out on the crowded platform a woman screamed.

A group of five or six uniformed policemen were surrounding a fallen man, a Brazil vet judging by the faded uniform he wore. Several were prodding him with shockrods and one cop was kicking him in the ribs.

"Remind me," said Gomez, "never to do whatever it was that *hombre* did."

Dan said, "They shouldn't be treating him like that."

"Don't tell them so," advised his father.

The speakers said, "We will open the doors, ladies and gentlemen, just as soon as a minor incident involving begging without a permit is settled."

The beggar cried out in pain, shook convulsively and then passed into unconsciousness. Three of the skyport officers took hold of him and dragged him away along the mosaic tile platform.

"Not a good place to work without a permit," observed Gomez as the doors finally hissed open.

Dan said, "But no officer should treat a suspected violator like—"

"And visitors from out of town shouldn't criticize them," said Jake. "Not too loudly anyway."

"Okay," said Dan, frowning, "all right."

"You've got an hour and a half after our skyliner takes off for Berlin before yours heads out for Greater LA," reminded Jake as they started along the platform toward the Europe Wing complex. "I don't want you getting into any sort of—"

"Hey, I'm not a kid. I got down here on my own, didn't need anybody to hold my hand or stick an electrotag on me," he told Jake. "I think I can manage to toddle back to the US Wing of this place on my own."

"Just be sure you don't stop to interfere with any local law enforcement operations."

"Actually, you know, I ought to be traveling to Berlin with you and Sid. I could really be a—"

"Back to school is where you're going," cut in his father.

"But helping you over there would be an educational experience, Dad."

Gomez said, "I doubt the SoCal State Police Academy would agree, *niño*."

Dan gave him a frowning look. "Don't you call me a kid, too."

"Cardigan, what a great blinking surprise running into you." Striding toward them across the vast domed room was the silver-haired Larry Knerr. "You're just the chap I'm most eager to interview."

"Go away," advised Jake.

"Seriously, my friend," continued the *GLA Fax-Times* newsman, "this has become a very important news story now. What I really could use is your reactions to the death of Beth Kittridge. Emotional stuff on that and then some shrewd speculation as to who is behind the whole—"

Jake took hold of the young man's arm just above the elbow. "I'm not fully convinced that you and China Vargas weren't involved somehow in setting me up. Right now, though, I have something more important to—"

"Set you up? Good lord, man, are you blinking paranoid?" Knerr struggled to break free of Jake's grip. "We hired you, remember? And, believe me, old man, we were as taken in by that Sparey woman same as you were. You must know that the Vargas family wouldn't be party to any sort of—"

"*Amigo,* I won't say this *cabrón* doesn't need some rattling," said Gomez to his partner, "but if you don't want to attract the law, you'd better cease this lively conversation."

Glancing around, Jake noted that two uniformed skyport officers were watching him from beside a decorative palm tree. "Yeah, you're right." He let go of the silverhaired newsman. "I've got no comment for the press. Goodbye."

Knerr took a few shaky steps back, rubbing at his arm. "I warned you before, Cardigan, that you'd be better off trying to get along with us." Turning, angry, he went walking away.

Watching him go, Dan asked, "How's he fit into all this?"

"I'm not exactly sure," answered Jake.

Dan was almost an hour out of Rio, heading home toward GLA, before Larry Knerr approached him.

The newsman had apparently been sitting in the forward section of the skyliner. He came ambling back, a glass clutched in his left hand, to halt in the aisle next to Dan's seat. "Well, here's another blinking coincidence," he said, chuckling. "Imagine your being on the same flight."

Dan looked up at him. "My father doesn't think much of you."

"I've noticed that, yes, and it upsets me. I can't, truly, understand why," said Knerr. "I've been making, after all, an enormous effort to ingratiate myself with the old boy."

"The point is—I'd prefer not to talk to you, Mr. Knerr."

"Is that being quite fair, young fellow? All I require from you is some background material." Knerr leaned down. "About what your dad is up to, what he intends to do over in Germany. And you knew Beth Kittridge, too, so you can give me your own impressions of this tragedy and—"

"I promised my father I wouldn't get into any trouble on my trip home," he said quietly. "So you'd better leave me alone, before I break my word."

"Lord, you're as cranky as your old man."

"Runs in the family."

Shaking his head, scowling, Knerr took a quick swig of his drink. "Very well, sonny boy, I'll leave you to your thoughts," he said. "But keep in mind that I may be able to help you some day."

"You may at that," said Dan.

═19═

IT WAS FOGGY in Berlin. A thick greyness surrounded the Sekunde Skyport and pressed against the plastiglass walls of the corridor leading to the customs area. The midnight city outside lay hidden.

Hunching his shoulders slightly, Gomez remarked, "I prefer tropical climes."

"You didn't much like them when we were hiking through Brazil."

"I mean to look at, *amigo*."

At the end of the corridor was posted a large gunmetal robot with a scanner built into his left hand. "Please have your passport cards ready," he repeated to the line of freshly disembarked passengers that included Jake and Gomez.

"Dan ought to be home in GLA by now," said Jake.

"How old do you think he is?" asked his partner.

"He's fifteen. I know how old my—"

"Allow me to rephrase that. How old do you *feel* he is?"

Jake admitted, "About ten or eleven I guess."

"He can fend for himself in most situations."

"Mein herr, your passport card, *bitte,"* requested the robot of Gomez, holding out his metal hand.

Gomez placed the card atop the scanner. He then stood shifting absently from foot to foot. "As I was saying, Jake, Dan is—"

"You are Gomez, Sid?" asked the customs robot.

"Also known as Sid Gomez, *sí.*"

"If you pass into the next room and wait by Doorway 16, Herr Gomez, please."

"Why am I doing that?"

"I have been instructed to convey the message. I can provide no details."

Shrugging, Gomez walked on into the large oval room.

When Jake presented his card, the robot gave him the same instructions.

Waiting in front of Doorway 16 were two men. The larger and elder was a blond man of about forty-five. *"Guten Abend,* Jake," he said cordially, holding out his hand.

Jake studied the big man's tanned face for a few seconds. "Rhinehart Spellman?"

"That's right. Welcome to Berlin."

"You still a sergeant with the *Hauptstädische Polizei?*"

"I'm an Assistant Inspector now," answered Spellman. He gestured at the lean dark man beside him. "This is my colleague, Lieutenant DeSelms."

Gomez inquired, "Is this more than a welcoming committee, Inspector?"

"Well, Jake and I do happen to be old friends. We worked together on two or three investigations that took me to Greater Los Angeles some years ago," he said. "Tonight, however, we're on official business."

"You arresting us?" asked Jake.

"Nein." Spellman shook his head. "We assume you're here because of the tragic death of Miss Kittridge and the two IDCA agents. Is that so, Jake?"

"Yeah, but—"

"Our superior, Chief Inspector Hauser, wishes to talk to you before you begin any investigation of the matter."

"Talk about what?" asked Jake.

"The fact that," replied the Assistant Inspector, "we have in custody the man who killed Beth Kittridge."

Inspector Hauser of the Berlin Metropolitan Police was a plump, pinkish man of fifty. He was standing, widelegged, next to the holographic projection platform at the center of his office. The office was high in the Polizei Hauptquartier building just off the Kurfürstendamm. "We have as yet, gentlemen, not released anything about this to the news media," he was saying. "I am assured by Assistant Inspector Spellman here that you will not discuss this with anyone on the outside."

"Can you tell us how you tracked this man down?" Jake was straddling a metal chair near the circular platform.

"Actually, he came to us," replied Hauser, who was holding a controlbox in his hand. He pushed a sequence of keys.

The platform produced a crisp popping sound. Ten seconds later a lifesize tridimensional holographic image of a tall, thin young man materialized. He wore a shabby grey suit and his sandy blond hair was shortcropped. His left eyelid drooped nearly shut and two fingers of his right hand were folded in on his palm. He sat very straight in a metal chair and his knees and ankles were pressed tight together.

"Repeat your name, please," requested an unseen voice.

"Will Goldberg."

"Age?"

"Twenty nine."

"Why did you kill these people?"

"I didn't intend to kill anyone but her."

"You mean Beth Kittridge?"

"Yes. She was my one true love."

Jake stood up. "Who the hell is this guy?"

"Watch a few more minutes, Herr Cardigan," suggested the Chief Inspector.

". . . and fell in love at SoCal Tech," continued Goldberg, still sitting stiffly. "We became very close friends."

"You slept together?"

"Oh, no. We never did anything carnal, because that would have been wrong. Beth often suggested that we try . . . certain things. But I wouldn't do anything of that nature. It would have spoiled the—"

"This asshole was never a friend of Beth's," shouted Jake, circling the platform and jabbing a finger at the lifesize image.

"Let's hear his spiel." Gomez was leaning against a desk.

". . . for several years I was Beth's closest friend. Then that terrible person became her lover."

"Whom do you mean, Herr Goldberg?"

A spasm of pain passed through his lean body. "I don't wish to speak his name."

"Jake Cardigan?"

"Yes, that's the man. He defiled her, stole my Beth from me and ruined her." Both his eyes were tight shut. "I pleaded with her to renounce the sinful life she lived with him, yet she refused. When I realized that she would never give him up, I knew there was only one way to save her immortal soul."

"You mean by killing her?"

"Yes, her body, you see, had to be sacrificed in order to save her spirit." He smiled contentedly. "She's safe now."

"How did you do this, Herr Goldberg?"

"I happen to be an expert in the field of robotics. That's one of the many interests my darling Beth and I shared. I began constructing the android replica of . . . of that evil man several months ago. I knew that the day would come when I would have the opportunity of using it to purify her."

"How did you get this android to Berlin?"

"Friends helped me smuggle it in. It was in several parts," replied the young man. "I reassembled the android here and added the explosive charge."

"Your android was very much like the kamikazes used by the Tek cartels, wasn't it?"

"Certainly, yes. I based mine on theirs. Although my andy was, from all the accounts I've studied, much more sophisticated and efficient."

"You maintain that you aren't working for one of the Tek cartels?"

"I am working only to do God's blessed will, sir."

The image faded and was gone.

Jake turned toward Chief Inspector Hauser. "This guy is a fake," he said evenly.

The plump man gave a disagreeing shake of his head. "Not at all, Herr Cardigan."

"Every aspect of his story checks out, Jake," added Spellman. "We even have the three fellows who helped him get the android into the country."

Jake shook his head. "I don't care who or what you've got. Will Goldberg was never a friend of Beth Kittridge."

"But he was," said Hauser calmly. "We have already done considerable preliminary work on this matter. Goldberg and the Kittridge woman did attend SoCal Tech in your own Greater Los Angeles together, Herr Cardigan. They were, according to several reliable witnesses, very close and intimate friends."

"They weren't, not at all."

Spellman coughed into his fist. "What makes you so certain, Jake?"

"Beth told me about the men she'd been involved with."

"Perhaps she had some reason for keeping the relationship with Goldberg to herself."

"Meaning what, Rhinehart?" Jake strode over to Spellman, stood facing him. "Damn it, I knew her better than anyone. She never lied to me, never kept anything important back from me."

"So you believed."

"No, so I *knew!*"

"Jake, this fellow's story seems to hold up so far," persisted the Assistant Inspector. "We're still investigating certain aspects, of course, yet I must tell you that—"

"C'mon, you don't really accept the idea that a lone fanatic is responsible for the killings?" demanded Jake. "You can't possibly think it's simply a coincidence that the Tek cartels benefit from Beth's murder?"

"A good investigator doesn't approach a case with too many preconceptions, Herr Cardigan," reminded Hauser.

"Yeah, and a good investigator doesn't get hoodwinked by an obvious fake."

"Am I wrong in believing that you come to us fresh from being hoodwinked in Rio?" inquired Hauser. "Perhaps you ought to—"

"Let me talk to Goldberg," requested Jake.

"That's not possible at present."

"I can persuade him to tell the truth."

"We're holding him at our psychiatric facility. After he's been processed there, perhaps it—"

"How long is that going to take?"

"A few more days."

"In a few more days, Inspector Hauser, the real killers may be—"

"I have, because Inspector Spellman spoke so highly of you, gone against my better judgment, Herr Cardigan, and shared highly confidential information with you," Hauser said. "I sincerely hope that you will now take my advice and refrain from pursuing this matter further on your own."

Jake took a slow breath in, then slowly exhaled. "I appreciate your sharing all this with us," he said. "We won't tell anyone what we've heard while we're in town."

"Then you intend to remain in Berlin?"

Jake grinned. "For awhile, yeah."

$\equiv$ 20 $\equiv$

THE BLONDE YOUNG woman was sitting on the neoleather sofa in the parlor of their suite at the Hotel Palast when they walked in. She wore a black slaxsuit, black gloves and boots. There was a silver lazgun dangling from her right forefinger.

"I'm not all that keen on waiting around," she informed them. "Where the heck were you dimwits?"

Gomez eyed her, booting the hall door shut behind him with his heel. "Are you part of the decor, miss?"

"That's right, Gomez, you're supposed to be the smartass of the team." She spun the gun twice before flipping it away into her shoulder holster. "You were due to check in several hours ago. So what happened?"

Jake sat down opposite her. "Here's how we'll run this conversation," he said. "You tell us who the hell you are."

"Don't you know?"

"Outside of the fact that you're someone who's working very hard to impress us, I haven't any idea who you might be," he admitted.

"She has to be either clever or influential to have gotten in here," observed Gomez.

"I'm both," she assured them. "My name is Jenny Keaton."

Gomez wandered over to an armchair. "You drop that name as though you expect us to snap our fingers and exclaim, 'Ah, of course!' "

She was frowning. "Didn't Bascom warn you to watch out for me?"

Jake shook his head. "Nope."

"He didn't tell you about the fracas I had with Deputy Director Waugh?"

"Would that be Gerald H. Waugh of the United States Internal Security Office?"

"Well, yes. Who else?"

Gomez snapped his fingers. "Ah, of course," he said. "Waugh and Bascom are longtime chums. The ISO must be the US government agency that hired Cosmos to dig into this."

"That's exactly what happened," Jenny said. "I assumed you two knew whom you were working for."

"Bascom is ofttimes fond of keeping us in the

dark as to who our client might be," explained Gomez.

"Well, I told Waugh that I was perfectly capable of handling this myself," continued the young woman. "I didn't need a couple of moronic excops stumbling around Berlin, making buffoons of themselves and generally getting in my way."

Gomez smiled at her. "I bet you never studied public relations or diplomacy in school."

Jake asked, "You work with Internal Sec, Miss Keaton?"

"Obviously. The ISO was assigned the job of investigating the possibility that someone in the International Drug Control Agency might be involved in some way with these assassinations."

"You have any credentials?"

Sighing impatiently, she yanked out an ID packet and tossed it at him. "Here."

"Did you drop in on us to suggest we work together on this, *chiquita?*" inquired Gomez. "That we pool our resources and become a jolly team dedicated to—"

"Far as I know, you don't have any resources." She stood up. "No, I simply came by to warn you bozos."

Jake had finished looking over her IDs. "These are authentic." He flipped the packet in her direction. "Says you're an Assistant Director with the ISO. I keep getting mixed up—is that higher or lower than an Associate Director?"

"Lower." She slipped the IDs away inside her coat.

"You were going to warn us about something," prompted Gomez.

"To stay the heck out of my way," she said. "I had to cajole and yell to get this assignment. I don't intend to let either of you foul me up."

"Could it be," suggested Jake, getting slowly to his feet, "that the reason Deputy Director Waugh brought in an outside agency is because he doesn't quite trust everybody in his own outfit either?"

"He trusts me."

"But you had to cajole and yell to get sent here."

"Okay, you know how Tek money can sometimes reach pretty high," she said. "Right now—well, certain people in Washington are suspicious of each other. Personally I don't for a second believe that anyone in our agency is unreliable."

"You couldn't convince Waugh of that, huh?"

"Not completely," she admitted. "But I did get him to agree to let me work on the assassination case. Independently and entirely on my own." She crossed to the door. "To sum up, gents—stay clear, please, of me and I'll stay clear of you. Keep in mind, too, that if I find out you're crooked, I won't hesitate to run you in."

"That's understood." Jake opened the door for her. "And we'll do the same for you."

At dawn Jake tapped on the door of Gomez's room. Then he opened it and went in.

Gomez sat up. "Trouble, *amigo?*"

"Nope, I'm just letting you know that I'm heading out."

"This is, if my body clock is functioning properly, an ungodly hour in the morning."

"Around six A.M.," said Jake. "I didn't want you to find me absent and think I was off frequenting some Berlin Tek parlor."

"So where are you going?"

"To talk to Will Goldberg."

"I had the impression the Berlin cops don't want you to do that."

"When Spellman was out in Greater LA some years ago, I did him a couple of favors."

"And you've convinced him he owes you one?"

Jake nodded. "Spellman's going to sneak me into the hospital where they're holding Goldberg."

"I'll probably loll around in bed for at least another hour," his partner told him. "Then I'll venture forth to look up some of my old contacts in town."

"You have contacts just about everywhere."

"Despite what Jenny Keaton says, I'm a very personable and winning fellow," Gomez said.

"And the last time I worked a case in Berlin I was generous with my payoffs and bribes. Which is why so many local informers will remember me fondly."

—=21=—

THE FOG PERSISTED. The early morning sky over Berlin was thick with it as Inspector Spellman piloted the police skycar toward the psychiatric detention center.

"I don't know how you might feel about attending," he said to Jake, "but there's to be a memorial service for Beth Kittridge and the two IDCA agents this afternoon."

"Where and when?"

"It's to be held at the American Embassy Chapel at three."

"Maybe I'll go."

"We aren't exactly close friends, Jake," said the police officer as they flew through the misty morning. "But I've known you for many years."

"Before and after my fall from grace."

Spellman said, "You were obviously very hard hit by Miss Kittridge's death. It's possible that your strong feelings are getting in the way of your—"

"You mean if I wasn't temporarily goofy I'd accept the notion that Will Goldberg killed her?"

"Well, you might at least consider the facts more calmly than you have."

"The facts are that Beth was killed by a kamikaze android, the kind the Teklords use," Jake said, "and Goldberg is a phony dragged in to divert suspicion."

"We have, as I've told you, considered those possibilities, Jake."

"And then gone right back to this bullshitter."

"Our forensic staff is going over the fragments of the android now." Leaning forward, Spellman tapped out a landing pattern. "So far they've found nothing to indicate that the dupe of you wasn't built originally in Southern Cal."

"Maybe it was built there, maybe Goldberg put the damn thing together singlehanded," said Jake. "But that asshole was never a friend of Beth's."

"Our inquiries indicate that he was."

"Have you sent anyone to Greater LA?"

"No, but we've had the GLA police conduct the necessary—"

"Hell, there's no use arguing about this," Jake told him as the skycar settled down on the roof of the multistoried black building near the Volkspark. "You're never going to convince me that Beth was having an affair with this religious fanatic. Nor that he went bonkers and decided to kill her because she was involved with me."

"The man is admittedly not rational, but that, in my view, gives weight to his story."

Jake said, "I appreciate your sneaking me in here."

"I'm hoping this unofficial visit will convince you that the true killer has been found and there's no need for you to linger in Berlin." Opening his door, he stepped out onto the misty landing area. "Here's an ID packet that shows you're Dr. Warren Steiner of the Frankfurt Krankenhaus Foundation."

Jake accepted the false identification papers. "You probably think I'd be more convincing posing as a patient," he said.

The Cafe Elektrisch was off the Marx-Engels Platz and next door to the Nazi Nostalgia Shop. Gomez, whistling quietly, paused to glance in the shop window at a display of Storm Trooper trading cards and then to scan a gloposter announcing an upcoming Hitlercon in Hamburg.

"Maybe I need a hobby," he told himself as he moved on and entered the small cafe.

There were fewer than ten patrons in the place and the only waiter, a fat android in lederhosen, lay flat on his back near the breakfast buffet. "Waiter's on the blink," called the thin, overcoated young Chinese who stood up and beckoned to Gomez with his metal right arm. "You'll have to serve yourself from the buffet."

Approaching the young man's table, Gomez said, "I came for information, Timecheck, not food."

As the informant settled back into his chair, he consulted one of the watches built into his arm. "Took your sweet time getting here, buddy," he observed. "I phoned you at 6:14 A.M. and here it is way past 6:31."

"I paused to dress." He sat down. "How come you're in Germany?"

"Seeing the world," replied Timecheck. "We, none of us, don't realize how little time we have. I made up my mind to do more sightseeing before I conk."

"You implied that you had some important news to sell."

"Have you had breakfast?" There was a large plate of food in front of him.

"A brief, hasty one enroute."

"Go fetch yourself some knackwurst and a side order of potato salad."

Gomez winced. "I favor oatmeal at this hour."

"There's another mistake many people make. Life is short and yet there's a multitude of different foods to consume. Yet we get in ruts and refuse to—"

"I never tire of oatmeal. Now what exactly is it you—"

"Can you imagine my surprise, chum, when I got wind that you were here in Berlin same as me." Timecheck tapped his metal arm and then brought it closer to his face. "My damn watch that shows California time is running four seconds slow again."

"Let's attend to business."

Timecheck filled a fork with purple cabbage. "Why don't you at least have a helping of strudel?"

"What do you know about the murder of Beth Kittridge?"

"I don't *know* a damn thing," replied Timecheck. "But I've sure *heard* some interesting stuff the past couple of days. You see, that's one of my strong suits, Gomez. I hear better than most anybody." He ate some cabbage. "I was going to take some spaetzle, too, but it looked a little too gummy. Just as I was consulting the waiter about it, his battery went flooey and he took a flop. Been sprawled there for about . . ." He pushed back the sleeve of his plaid overcoat to consult another watch face. ". . . about thirteen minutes and ten seconds. They're very casual and relaxed here. A waiter falls over, that doesn't cause any stress."

"Tell me," urged Gomez, "what you've heard."

Resting both elbows on the table top, Timecheck said, "This fellow Goldberg is a ringer."

"That conclusion we've already reached on our own."

"He's a washed-up electronics whiz with a serious Tek habit," continued the informant. "He *thinks* they're going to spring him in a short while and pay him a tidy sum." Timecheck laughed, shook his head, gathered another forkful of purple cabbage. "Actually, however, when they filled his brain with false memories to fool any possible police probes, they planted a little something extra."

"Such as?"

"Let's just say that Goldberg's time, unbeknownst to him, is pretty near run out," said Timecheck. "The guy really did attend school with Beth Kittridge, by the way, except they were never friends. That's one of the reasons, though, that they picked him to take the rap for this job. His background could be shuffled a little to make the romance angle plausible."

"Who's behind this?"

"Don't know yet. But it's got to be one of the bigger Tek cartels."

"Got anything else?"

Timecheck laughed again. "Would I charge you $2000 for what I've passed along thus far? Not likely, buddy."

"Well, then you better come up with another $1500 worth of information."

"Goldberg, the patsy, didn't build the sim of Jake," said the informant. "Who did? Well sir, to learn that you have only to go talk with the Amazing Otto."

"The Amazing Otto," echoed Gomez without much enthusiasm. "Who might he be?"

"A magician."

"And?"

"The guy knows who really constructed the killer andy." Timecheck gave him an address. "Go see him."

"I shall."

"But first why not try that strudel?"

Jake and Inspector Spellman descended through a glaring white silence, along white-walled corridors and over white tile flooring. At each level was stationed a large white-enameled medibot who checked their ID packets and then allowed them to move down to the next level.

"You can only talk to Goldberg for a few minutes," said Spellman quietly.

"That may be enough."

"And, obviously, you're not to threaten him in any way or use force."

"I understand, yeah."

"He's in a private room just around this next bend."

They entered another white corridor. About a third of the way down it a white door stood open.

"That his room?" asked Jake.

Spellman started running. *"Ja,* it is."

William Shatner

The room was furnished with a white bed and two white metal chairs. The bed linen lay in a tangle on the floor.

Will Goldberg was not there.

—≡ 22 ≡—

THE OLD MECHANIKER Schauplatz theater was
full of shadows and hollow echoes. As Gomez
made his way down the threadbare carpeting of
the center aisle toward the brightlit stage he
was aware of the mixed smells of damp, mold
and decay, along with the scent of freshmade
nearcaf.

Up on the stage sat a banquet table with a
dozen splendidly dressed men and women
around it.

A small greybearded man in a tuxsuit pushed
back his ornately carved chair and left the
table to walk to the footlights. "Herr Gomez, is
it?"

Gomez halted just short of the orchestra pit.
"You're the Amazing Otto?"

"I am, *ja.*" He bowed, then straightened and raised his metallic left arm. He plucked a bouquet of yellow roses out of the air. "Before this theater converted to android performers many years ago, I was the star attraction." He tossed the flowers high in the air and when they reached the apex of their climb, they vanished with a flash of golden light.

"Impressive." Gomez scanned the group seated around the table. "All the rest are androids, huh?"

"Ja, Herr Gomez. I'm the caretaker now and I don't like to breakfast alone," he explained. "But I also don't care for inane chatter, so I rarely activate them. Would you care to join me for a cup of nearcaf?"

"Much obliged, *sí."* He climbed the sidestairs onto the stage.

"Timecheck told me you were coming, and provided me with a portrait." In his metal hand now appeared a faxpic. "You've put on a little weight."

Gomez took the picture and studied it. "Only around the middle."

The Amazing Otto took hold of a handsome android actor by the collar of his tuxsuit and yanked him free of his chair. "We need your seat, Herr Baron."

The mechanical man hit the stage with a resounding thud.

Stepping over the fallen actor, Gomez seated himself next to an immobile redhaired young woman. "According to Timecheck, you have something to tell me," he said to the grey-bearded magician.

The Amazing Otto returned to his chair. "It could be highly dangerous for me to pass along what I know." He stared out into the shadowy theater. "So far, fortunately, only you and Timecheck are aware of the information I happen to possess. It is quite valuable."

"How valuable?"

The Amazing Otto pointed his metal forefinger at an empty cup. Steaming nearcaf came spouting out. "What I know is, I estimate, worth $5000." He handed him the cup.

"That's a very handy finger you have there."

"I have over 500 tricks and gadgets built into me," said the magician proudly. "No other performer in all of Germany, past or present, comes near that."

"Impressive," repeated Gomez. "For the price do we get the identity of the maker of the android that was used to kill Beth Kittridge?"

The magician sipped his imitation coffee. "I can tell you, *ja,* who built it," he promised.

"That's worth $3000 tops."

"Nein, $5000."

Shaking his head, Gomez started to rise up. "Looks like, then, we won't be—"

"$4500."

"$4000."

The Amazing Otto slumped slightly in his chair. "Very well, Herr Gomez."

"Was the kamikaze made here in Berlin?"

"*Ja,* near here. That's how I came to have knowledge of it."

"Who built the thing?"

The magician held up two metal fingers. "There were two of them, a couple," he answered. "That is to say, a married couple. At the moment they are touring in Switzerland, but until last week they—"

"You've talked quite enough this morning, old man." Directly across the table from him one of the androids stood up. He was holding a lazgun in his gloved right hand.

They found Will Goldberg in the Emergency Wing. The confessed killer was hooked up to a white medibed and had two white-enameled robots and a plump human doctor attending him.

The young man was writhing on the bed, eyes tight shut, teeth gnashing. His skin was a chalky grey, his breath was rattling in his chest.

Jake and Inspector Spellman were standing outside the room, looking in through the see-through plastiglass wall.

"What's wrong with him?" asked Jake.

Spellman touched the keyboard beneath the vidchart mounted on the wall. A report on the young man appeared on the greenish screen. "According to this, he's dying," he said after skimming it. "From a synthetic virus—what they call a timebomb virus."

"Something that was injected in him before he got here?"

"Yes, exactly. A week to ten days ago, judging from the prelim tests. It apparently just kicked in at five A.M. this morning."

"Can they save him?"

Spellman touched the keys again, then nodded at the medscreen. "See for yourself."

" 'Irreversible,' " he read.

"I wonder now if perhaps your theory about—"

"Maybe I can still find out something." Jake went striding to the door of the room and yanked it open.

"You can't go in there." The inspector hurried after him.

Jake pushed on in. He nudged aside a robot and stopped next to the bed. "Goldberg!"

"Please, stand away," ordered the heavyset blond human physician. "This man is in a critical condition."

Jake took hold of Goldberg's arm. "Listen— this is Jake Cardigan."

"I must ask you to leave," persisted the doctor.

"Stay out of my way," Jake advised him. He leaned closer to the dying man. "Goldberg, I'm Jake Cardigan. You're supposed to hate me."

The young man's eyelids fluttered, then opened slightly. "Jake . . ."

"Who hired you? Who's behind this?"

The young man opened his right eye wider,

stared up at Jake. "Doublecross," he said in a dry, gasping voice. "I trusted . . . sun . . . sun . . ."

"Who?" Jake shook him. "Who rigged this and crossed you?"

"Sands . . . sun . . ." He started making harsh choking noises, his body shook violently.

The doctor shoved Jake back, bending over Goldberg. "You idiot, now this man is dying!"

"He was dying before I got here."

"Sun . . ." Goldberg opened both eyes wide and struggled to sit up. "They fucked me good . . ."

The life went out of him. He sank back, sighing out breath and blood.

══ 23 ══

THE ANDROID ACTOR was tall and handsome. He smiled at both Gomez and the Amazing Otto, his lazgun held at waist level. "Herr Gomez, there is no need for me to kill *you,*" he assured him in his deep resonant voice.

"Well, I appreciate that," said Gomez, shifting nervously in his chair. "For all practical purposes, I'm simply an innocent bystander." He gestured awkwardly with his right hand, managing to smack the immobile android actress seated next to him. "Oops." Laughing apologetically, he grabbed her bare shoulder and straightened her in her chair.

"Who activated you?" the magician asked the android. "No one is supposed to fool with the actors stored in this—"

"The real issue is that they don't want you to talk about what you know," explained the handsome android. He rested his free hand on the table top as he stood there. The barrel of his silvery lazgun was aimed at the Amazing Otto.

"What do you mean?"

"Basically, Herr Otto, I refer to certain things you've chanced to learn about a particular kamikaze." The actor inclined his head in Gomez's direction. "As soon as I kill him, Herr Gomez, you can go on your way."

"Say, that's really gracious of you," Gomez told him, a nervous quiver in his voice. "Actually, as you know, since you've been sitting here all along, playing possum, as the saying goes, I haven't so far learned a blessed thing from the Amazing Otto." He made another sweeping gesture.

This time he whapped the android actress much harder. She went tilting far to the right, teetered, and then, before Gomez could catch her, fell clean off her chair.

That caused the android, as Gomez had anticipated, to glance in her direction.

Gomez threw himself backwards, causing his chair to tip over. He executed a deft somersault and then dived into the orchestra pit. He yanked out his stungun as he fell.

Rolling across the dusty floor, he popped to his feet.

Up on the stage the big andy was shoving

aside the fallen actress so that he could get down to the footlights.

Gomez fired his stungun up at him.

The handsome mechanism stopped dead, swayed, staggered and then tumbled back against the banquet table. Several dishes came bouncing to the floor and then the disabled android hit and lay still.

"Bueno," commented Gomez as he started to climb back onto the stage.

"People, you'll find, Herr Gomez, are harder to fool than mechanical actors." Two large men with slick cleanshaved heads had emerged from the wings stage left.

Each held a lazgun, and the huskier of the pair, the one who'd addressed Gomez, was making his way toward the edge of the stage.

"I should've considered the possibility of a backup," Gomez said up at him.

"Toss your gun onto the stage, *bitte,"* requested the big man as he squatted and pointed his lazgun down at him.

Frowning, Gomez moved his wrist back and prepared to surrender his weapon.

Just then streamers of crackling red fire started spewing out of both of the Amazing Otto's ears.

It took the attention of both the gunmen.

Gomez seized the opportunity to fire his stungun up at the squatting one.

The bald man gasped, sat down hard, rocked a few times and then stretched out flat and stiff.

Gomez boosted himself back up onto the boards of the stage.

The greybearded magician was just in the process of pulling a stungun out of thin air. He fired it at the still dazzled other gunman.

Stepping sideways, that one dropped his lazgun and knelt. He remained that way for roughly ten seconds before falling over facefirst.

"That was very invigorating," commented the Amazing Otto. "I haven't, I don't believe, performed the blazing ears illusion for nearly a decade."

"I'm glad you decided to revive it today," Gomez said. "Now let's sneak off to someplace quiet where you can tell me the rest of—"

"I'll come along, too." From out of the wings stage right came Jenny Keaton of the Internal Security Office.

The Chief Inspector pointed at Jake. "You had no right to be here," he said accusingly. "It is quite probable, Herr Cardigan, that you hastened the poor fellow's death."

They were in a stark white office, Jake, Spellman, the doctor who'd attended Will Goldberg and Chief Inspector Hauser.

Jake, who was sitting in a stiff white chair, said, "His death was arranged before he even turned himself in. Goldberg was never more than a diversion."

"I admit," said Hauser from behind the wide

metal desk he'd taken over, "that the circumstances of his death are suspicious."

"To say the least," said Jake. "They wanted to sidetrack you and the other investigating agencies. Long enough, anyway, to cover their tracks some."

"There is still the possibility, however, that the young man administered the fatal injection to himself," said Hauser. "Making this, then, nothing more than the suicide of the guilty person."

Jake shrugged. "Suicides usually don't complain about being doublecrossed," he said. "I'd bet that Goldberg was surprised by what was happening to him."

"He apparently talked a little before he expired," said Chief Inspector Hauser.

"This man virtually shook the words out of him," accused the portly physician. "In my opinion he—"

"Yes, fine, doctor." The Chief Inspector turned to Spellman. "What exactly did Goldberg say at the end?"

"That he'd been doublecrossed, that they'd fucked him," he replied. "He also mumbled something about sun and sand."

"What do you think he was alluding to with that?" Hauser inquired of Jake.

"Probably a dying hallucination. He thought he was out in the desert somewhere. Sun, sand."

"The actual word he spoke was *sands,*" offered the doctor. "With an S."

Hauser nodded at Jake. "Could that have been, Herr Cardigan, a reference to Bennett Sands?"

Jake shrugged again. "Bennett Sands is dead and gone."

"Suppose, however, that the word he used was s-o-n and not s-u-n," suggested Hauser. "Perhaps Will Goldberg tried, as he was dying, to warn you that some of Sands' followers meant to harm your son."

"That doesn't seem likely to me."

The portly doctor said, "If Sands is a person, then the patient was talking about Sands' son and not this man's."

"How does that strike you, Herr Cardigan?"

"The only problem there, Inspector, is that Sands didn't have a son. Only a daughter."

Spellman said, "If you'd cooperate with us now, Jake, instead of holding back, it would help."

"I don't know what he was trying to convey, beyond the fact that he'd been set up," Jake told him, standing. "Are you folks going to charge me with anything?"

"Not at the present," said Hauser. "In fact, it might be a good idea if you left Berlin now."

"Until I got here you were all satisfied that Goldberg was the one you wanted. Now you—"

"Not satisfied, Herr Cardigan, but simply checking out the facts." Hauser rose, too.

Jake walked over to the door of the office. "Thanks for your help, Rhinehart. I hope I haven't screwed up your career too seriously." Nodding at them, he left.

=24=

GRUNTING AND MUMBLING, Gomez succeeded in getting the heavier of the unconscious gunmen up over his shoulder. "A waste of time, *chiquita,*" he informed Jenny.

She was dragging the other stunned gunman across the stage by his armpits. "I didn't have a very high opinion of you to begin with," the blonde agent told him. "But I didn't realize how slipshod you—"

"Running a check on these goons isn't going to enlighten you." He followed her into the wings, legs wobbling some. "Smartest thing to do is just leave them here."

"On the contrary, I'm darn certain that—"

"They're freelancers, hired for this one job."

The Amazing Otto, bringing up the rear,

urged, "We ought to get out of this theater as soon as possible. They may send more killers looking for me, *nein?*"

"I'd have fled several minutes ago," answered Gomez. "But I'm obliged to humor Miss Keaton, since she is, in a way, my employer at the moment."

"This is all standard procedure, Gomez." Dumping her unconscious lout beside the rear door, she drew her stungun. Cautiously she opened the heavy door.

After listening for half a minute, Jenny ventured out into the foggy alley.

"Things are okay out here," she called finally.

Gomez grunted and mumbled some more as he hefted his thug outside.

Jenny's skyvan was parked across the alley, its slick black surface speckled with mist. "Toss him in," she instructed.

"Yes, ma'am." Gomez lugged the big man over and dumped him into the passenger compartment she'd opened.

"Would you go back and fetch the other one now, please?"

"Caramba," he remarked as he returned for the second load.

The magician was standing in the open doorway, staring carefully out. "Are there any more of them lurking around, Herr Gomez?"

"Nary a one. Zip on over and hop into the van." Gomez decided to drag the second gunman rather than carry him. "We'll fly around for awhile and finish our chat."

"What took you so long?" Jenny climbed into the driveseat. "This guy's lighter."

"*Verdad,* but I didn't have a fractured spine when I hauled the first lout."

He hefted the gunman up into the skyvan, got him arranged on the floor next to his cohort.

Timidly the Amazing Otto scrambled in and took a seat as far from the sprawled thugs as he could get. "I have decided, Herr Gomez," he announced, "that what I know must be worth considerably more than $5000."

"Possibly it is." He settled next to Jenny in the foremost passenger seat. "Miss Keaton's agency will no doubt make up the difference between your new asking price and the $4000 that you and I already agreed on."

After making a rude noise, Jenny guided the skyvan up into the grey morning.

While Jake was on the vidphone with the Cosmos Detective Agency in Greater LA, the image of the staff robot he'd been talking to was abruptly replaced with that of Walt Bascom himself.

The agency head was looking especially frazzled and rumpled. "Why are you hobnobbing with a machine rather than me, my lad?" he inquired.

"Since it's the middle of the night where you are, I figured you were safely home by now."

"I rarely sleep. What were you calling about?"

Jake was sitting in one of the tapproof booths in his hotel lobby. "First, Walt, I want to know more about a lady named Jenny Keaton."

"A hoyden, a tough cookie, a gadfly on the backside of polite espionage and—"

"She claims we're working for her agency."

"In a manner of speaking, yes," admitted the Cosmos chief. "The ISO wants an impartial investigation of those Berlin assassinations."

"Apparently they don't trust the International Drug Control Agency or themselves."

"People in the government get that way." Bascom, yawning, rubbed his eyes, scratched an armpit. "There isn't that spirit of openness, trust and fairplay that you Cosmos ops enjoy each and every—"

"Keaton persuaded Deputy Director Waugh to let her work on this anyway, according to her. Is that what actually happened?"

Bascom nodded. "She's a tough cookie, as I mentioned earlier, and very persuasive."

"Suggest to your pal Waugh that we don't want her getting underfoot."

"You've met her then?"

"She introduced herself to us, yeah."

"Surely you and Gomez weren't intimidated

by someone who weighs in at about 110 pounds and—"

"Not intimidated, just annoyed," said Jake. "Next I wanted the robot to run a thorough background check on the late Will Goldberg."

"The confessed killer?"

"That Will Goldberg. How'd you hear about him? The Berlin police haven't as yet released any—"

"I'm a detective, too, remember? But I didn't know he was dead."

"He died a few hours ago, by way of a planted timebomb virus."

"You obviously don't believe this lad was the real killer."

"Nope."

"Neither do I. Anything else you need from us?"

"When he realized he'd been doublecrossed, Goldberg managed to say something to me," said Jake. "He seemed to be trying to warn me about Bennett Sands' son."

Bascom scowled thoughtfully. "If Sands had a son, I suppose the fellow might well be pissed off at you," he said. "Before you got on Sands' trail most of the world thought of him as a simple everyday multimillionaire tycoon. You linked the guy with the Hokori Tek cartel and sundry other—"

"Could there be a son somewhere—legit or otherwise?"

"Not that I know of, but we'll sure dig into that," promised his boss.

"There's one more thing," said Jake. "I just talked to Dan and he seems to be doing well. But I was thinking—"

"Cosmos already has a team looking after him, Jake, although your son isn't aware of it," said Bascom. "I initiated that myself."

"Thanks, Walt."

"Are you and Gomez making any progress so far?"

"Sid may be, but right now I feel as though I'm pretty much standing still," admitted Jake.

— 25 —

GOMEZ WAS SITTING deep in an armchair in the parlor of their suite when Jake returned. "I've led a blameless life," he said.

"Right. You've been an example to all who know you."

"And yet fate keeps dumping a succession of meanminded feisty women in my path. Looney reporters, killcrazy spies, snide government agents."

"You're upset about Jenny Keaton?"

"*Sí*, she's the latest thorn in my side."

Jake sat on the edge of the sofa. "Run into her again?"

Gomez replied, "That I did." He told him about his tracking down the Amazing Otto, about the attempt to kill the magician and about Jenny's intruding at the tag end of things.

"How'd she know about Otto?" asked Jake.

"She was pursuing, so she says, an independent tip."

"Sure she wasn't just pursuing you?"

"I know when I'm being tailed—especially by someone in a huge black skyvan," Gomez assured him. "Anyhow, this *mujer* then insisted that we—make that me. She insisted that I heft these two huge lunks into her van. She's got the damn crate crammed full of the latest in criminological gadgets."

"She ran checks on them?"

"*Sí,* hooked them up to a retscan machine, got their fingerprints and DNA patterns. Maybe even took their temperatures. Sent it all to Crime Central in Washington, DC." Gomez sank further into his chair. "Care to guess the result of all that?"

"These guys have no provable links with any of the Tek cartels. They're well known, though, as hoods-for-hire who'll work for anybody who pays their price," replied Jake. "They were hired to knock off the Amazing Otto before he talked and probably have no idea who their client was."

"Bingo."

Jake asked, "What did the magician finally have to tell you?"

"Sell me," he corrected. "He knows a married couple name of Boneca, Miguel and Roma

Boneca. These two operate something called the Puppenspiel Roving Theatre with a cast of electronic puppets."

"They're the ones who built the android simulacrum of me?"

"So swears Otto," said his partner. "The Bonecas have a flat a few blocks from the theater where he's the caretaker. He drops in on them now and then and a couple weeks back, by chance, he discovered that they were working on this replica of you. It didn't mean much to him then, but he thought differently after he saw the vidnews footage of . . . of what happened."

"You can say 'footage of Beth's getting killed,'" Jake told him. "I won't rush out and hook up to a Brainbox."

"Hey, I'm on your side, *amigo,*" reminded Gomez.

Jake said, "I know. Sorry."

"The Amazing Otto also mentioned that he suspects the Bonecas have done some shady jobs like this in the past, too."

"Are they still in Berlin?"

"They've been touring Switzerland since the day of the killings. I have a copy of their itinerary."

"You better get over there soon as you can."

"Aren't you coming along?"

"I want to stay in Berlin a little longer, see if I can trace Goldberg's activities."

"The local cops may frown on that."

"Yep, they may."

Gomez sighed. "In a moment of lunacy, I agreed to let Jenny Keaton work alongside us on this next phase of things," he confessed. "I didn't know I'd be alone with her amidst the snowcapped—"

"I checked her out with Bascom. He says she's exactly what she claims."

"You find out anything else about the lady?"

"She weighs 110 pounds."

"At least I outweigh her." Gomez sighed again.

The fog had given way to rain, a light prickly rain that drifted down across the afternoon.

Jake, hands thrust deep in his trouser pockets, walked once again slowly along the stretch of Unter den Linden across from the American Embassy chapel.

The sidewalk over there was thick with people, a noisy tangle of mourners, officials and gawkers. Uniformed city police were trying to get them sorted out.

Hovering over the rainswept street were three news camvans, the largest from Newz, Inc. Jake had spotted at least two dozen reporters, both human and robot, working on the ground.

Slowing, he halted next to a decorative linden tree that was made of neocon.

Skycars were gliding down, trying to land

and let out passengers. The air above the row of grey embassy buildings was cluttered with more vehicles, some attempting to reach the ground, others simply hovering to catch a glimpse of what was happening down below.

Jake, he realized now, felt colder than he should have. It was a deep coldness that seemed to come from within him.

"There's no need," he decided, "for me to go in there."

He didn't want to say goodbye to Beth this way.

From out of the chapel now spilled the mournful sound of amplified organ music. The memorial service was about to start.

"I lost her twice," he was thinking.

Down in Mexico when the android replica of Beth had sacrificed herself to save him. And again now—the real Beth this time.

"Jesus," he said aloud.

A wedge of people went surging forward, trying to force their way inside the already crowded chapel.

"A mistake to come here." He started walking away.

A thin young man in a long dark overcoat, bareheaded, came running over from across the way. "Herr Cardigan?"

"Yeah?" said Jake, tensing.

The young man handed him a folded slip of

paper. Then he backed, spun on his heel and went hurrying away through the misty rain.

Jake unfolded the note.

There was a single line printed on it—"She's still alive."

— 26 —

GOMEZ, CARRYING A single suitcase, made his way through the crowded main building of the Berlin Skyport. He was whistling softly, smiling now and then at a narrowly avoided collision with someone.

He was a hundred or so yards from Gate 227, when the overhead speakers announced, "Last call for Skyliner Flight S-09 for Bern, Switzerland. Boarding at Gate 227."

Kicking up his pace, Gomez hurried to the gate in question. "Good afternoon, *chiquita*."

Jenny Keaton, arms folded, blackbooted foot resting on the smallest of her three suitcases, was standing close beside the gate. "Didn't I mention earlier, Gomez, that I really don't like to be kept waiting?"

"You did, *sí,*" he acknowledged while showing his ticket to the silverplated robot at the gate. "The reason I remember that is—because I treasure every single word that falls from your lovely lips and I preserve them in the scrapbook of my memory."

"You truly are full of crap," observed the Internal Security Office agent. She nodded down at her luggage. "Could you, maybe, lend a hand with some of this?"

He grabbed up two of them. "I had assumed you were too fiercely independent to want help of any kind."

Following him up along the boarding ramp, Jenny said, "Why are you making those annoying groaning noises?"

"Oh, it's nothing, *bonita,*" he replied. "Ever since I strained my back lugging around those dazed goons for you, the lifting of several hundred pounds of superfluous baggage tends to cause me dreadful pain. But don't let it bother you."

"You're worse than the reports say."

"I strive to be, *sí.*"

A pair of pretty blonde android attendants welcomed them aboard and guided them to their seats midway in the skyliner.

After the luggage was stowed, Jenny settled into a window seat. "There's something I'd like to discuss with you, Gomez."

He was rubbing at a spot low on his back. "Go ahead."

"It's about Cardigan."

"If you have any questions about Jake, ask Jake."

"I simply don't think the man should be working on this case."

"The way I understand it, you don't think I should be either."

"But you're simply an annoying nitwit," she told him. "Cardigan, though, is much too emotionally upset to be at all objective about—"

"I've worked with Jake, off and on, for a long time," he told her. "He's got a temper, sure, but he's a damn good investigator and—"

"You know it's standard practice to take an agent off a case that has anything to do with someone he was closely involved with."

"That's not the way the Cosmos Agency does business," he said. "And now, in the interest of smooth sailing, I suggest that you quit nagging and change the topic."

"I'm not a nag," she argued. "Anyone with more than a peanut for a brain would realize that. Making useful suggestions doesn't—"

"Cease this," said Gomez quietly.

Jenny eyed him for a few seconds, then turned away to stare out the window.

The gaunt young man in the long black overcoat stumbled.

Jake, the slip of paper clutched in his hand, was a half block behind him. He slowed now, waiting for the young man to regain his balance and continue on his way.

The rain was growing heavier and immediately ahead of him a heavyset blonde woman clicked on her forcefield umbrella.

Jake's quarry was moving again, hurrying in a longlegged, jittery way. The skirt of his black overcoat flapped and billowed.

From a sausage shop on Jake's right a plump man came hurrying. He clutched a large plyo-wrapped parcel of soywurst, and engraved on his bald, polished head was a bloodred swastika.

Up ahead the thin young man went scurrying around a corner.

Jake opened his hand and read the note again. "She's still alive."

He wanted that to be true. And if Beth were alive, he had to find her.

"But she can't be," he told himself.

He'd seen her die, seen the damn explosion on the damn vidscreen.

"That could've been faked," he reminded himself inside his head.

Unlikely, though. Just because you wanted something to be true, that sure as hell didn't mean it was. Beth's murder and the deaths of the others had all been investigated. By the Berlin police and by several United States agencies.

"But they haven't been investigated by me."

The young man in the black overcoat had

157

entered a small park. A rundown, weedy square with a rusted metallic arch rising up at its center. Spelled out on the arch in dim, dusty plazbulbs was UNTERGRUNDSTADT.

Jake could hear the rusty metal gate creak open from across the way.

The man he was following pushed through the old gate, headed down the shadowy stairway beneath the arch.

When Jake reached the staircase, he heard footsteps come echoing up from underground.

Easing his stungun out of his shoulder holster, he slipped it into his jacket pocket and kept his fingers around the grip.

The metallic steps were part of a nonfunctioning escalator system that descended deep under the streets of Berlin. Every few yards a pale ball of yellow light floated, barely pushing back the surrounding darkness.

There was a thick smell of damp earth all around and a prickly chill hanging in the air.

Halting after he'd been climbing down for a few minutes, Jake listened. He could still hear the footfalls down below him as someone moved deeper into the rundown underground town.

After he'd dropped one more level down, he heard noise and saw lights off beyond the stairway. People were laughing, a robopiano was playing. The German words for food, sausage, beer and sex floated in the air, spelled out in twisted tubes of colored light.

He caught a glimpse of the young man as he ducked into a narrow saloon. The name scrawled over the neobrick entrance in glochalk was MAULWURF CLUB.

His right hand clutching the stungun in his pocket, Jake pushed the swing doors open with his left.

The room beyond was small, cold, smelling of mold and decay. All but one of its ten small tables were empty and behind the bar stood a large robot bartender who'd long ago been painted crimson.

There was no sign of the young man Jake had been trailing.

Occupying the table nearest the doorway was a pinkfaced moustached man in a grey suit. His feathery blond hair was parted neatly in the middle and he wore a pair of rimless blue-tinted spectacles.

Raising his copper tankard, he smiled at Jake. "Welcome, Herr Cardigan. We have some good news for you," he said. "*Ja*, some very good news."

$=27=$

THE DAY HAD dawned bright and clear in the Santa Monica Sector of Greater Los Angeles. The skybus let Dan Cardigan off at the edge of the five acre campus of the SoCal State Police Academy and went climbing back up into the brightening morning. Since it was so early, Dan was the only cadet to disembark.

He showed his ID packet to the robot guard at the high plastiglass gates and was admitted. Dan strode along a wide pathway that cut up across a stretch of fakegrass, passed the dorms and took him finally to the domed Reference and Research Wing.

The chromeplated guardbot at the entrance made an amused sound. "Exams are still two weeks off, Cadet Cardigan," he pointed out.

"You can't do too much studying, Casey."

Inside the early morning building Dan hurried up a ramp to the second level. He paused at a door marked BACKGROUND & ID, glancing around. He had the corridor to himself and, after taking a slow, careful breath, he entered the large room.

A big copperplated robot was sitting, huge feet resting on a packing crate, in a wicker rocking chair. "Geeze, here comes more trouble," he observed.

"Nope, I just need a small favor, Rex."

Rex/GK-30 swung his metallic feet to the floor. "Do you know how many strings I had to pull to get a soft job like this one, Daniel? If I keep letting you sneak in here to use the—"

"This won't take more than five minutes. Especially if you quit arguing about it and help."

"My problem—one of them anyway—is that I'm too darn amiable." The rocker creaked as he rose up out of it. "I knew your dad back when I used to work over at—"

"What I'd like is all the information you have on a man named Larry Knerr," Dan told him. "Currently he's working for the *GLA Fax-Times.*"

"That rag." Rex/GK-30 went lumbering over to the bank of infoscreens on the righthand wall of the high, wide room. "They don't even run a challenging crossword puzzle. I can always finish it in under three minutes."

"What's important about Larry Knerr?" inquired a young woman's voice.

Turning, Dan saw a slim darkhaired girl standing in the doorway and grinning in at him.

"Get in here, Molly, and shut the damn door," Dan said. "What the hell are you doing—"

"Well, I saw you go sneaking by my dorm window," explained Molly Fine, who was nearly a year older than Dan. "Slipping into my cadet uniform, I followed you. Curiosity."

"Go away," he suggested.

"You just now invited me in."

"Actually I was inviting you to stop hollering Larry Knerr's name up and down the hall," said Dan. "I'm not supposed to be using these—"

"It'll be my toke in a sling if anyone tumbles," added the robot. "If I wasn't such a softie, I'd give you both the old heave-ho."

Molly eased closer to Dan. "Who exactly is Larry Knerr?"

"Someone I'm interested in."

"Someone you met down in Brazil?"

Dan turned away from her. "Why do you keep nosing into my—"

"I'm your good friend, is why. Your pal, a helping hand in time of need. Stuff like that."

"No, you're not. I don't much like you and you don't much like me."

"I see through your act, Dan," Molly assured

him. "You pretend not to care for me because
you feel obliged to go on acting as though you
were still smitten with Nancy Sands. But, honestly now, she's at school way the heck over in
France and you're here in GLA. She hasn't
even communicated with you in any shape or
form for nearly two and a half weeks either."

He scowled at the darkhaired girl. "How do
you know that?"

"I'm a detective."

"You're a police cadet. One with a morbid
interest in my personal business."

She shrugged, then rubbed her hands together. "Let's get to work, shall we?"

"Okay, shooing you off is too much trouble
and I'm in a hurry." He crossed over to the
robot. "Rex, see what you can dig up about
Knerr."

The big robot nodded at one of the chest-high
screens. "While you two lovebirds were bicker-
ing, I located his file."

The lefthand side of the screen showed a se-
lection of head shots of the silverhaired Knerr.
On the right printed information was crawling
by.

"Now there's a coincidence for you," remarked Molly, touching the button that halted
the crawl and then tapping a line of the copy on
the screen. "This Knerr, before signing up with
the Vargas news empire, used to be employed
by the highly successful Ampersand Vidpix
Studios."

"So?" asked Dan.

She shook her head and made a disappointed sound. "Don't you know who used to own most of Ampersand?"

"No, nope."

"The late Bennett Sands, father of your uncommunicative girlfriend, noted business tycoon and notorious Teklord cohort," said Molly. "Sands wasn't exactly a chum of your dad's either."

Frowning, Dan read over the information on the screen. "Sands is dead, but . . ."

"We're going to have to dig a lot deeper in Knerr's background," decided Molly. "Might also be a good idea to start tailing the guy. I'm not sure if we're ready to try any electronic surveillance, but—"

"We aren't going to do a damn thing," Dan informed her. *"I'm* going to work on this, *you're* going to quit as of now and leave me entirely alone."

Molly laughed. "No, I'm not."

— ☰ 28 ☰—

THE PLUMP PINKFACED man gestured at the other chair at his table. "May I buy you a beer, Herr Cardigan?"

"No." Jake sat, placed the note on the table top. After smoothing it out, he slid it over toward the man. "You sent this?"

"Ja," he replied, smiling.

"Who were you referring to?"

"We are both aware that I meant Beth Kittridge. You certainly wouldn't have come to such a disreputable sector of Berlin if you hadn't known I—"

"Okay, enough bullshit," cut in Jake, leaning forward. "Who are you—what do you know?"

Smiling more broadly, he answered, "I'm Ulrich Kreuz. The journalist?"

"Haven't heard of you. Sorry."

Kreuz sighed. "Apparently I'm not especially well known outside my native land." He paused to sip at his tankard of foamy beer. "I'm a reporter with the Zeitung Agency and—"

"If you suckered me here just to get an interview about Beth, you—"

"Nein, you don't comprehend. My news service represents the more conservative factions in Germany, factions that are currently out of power," explained the reporter. "I brought you here to pass along some information, Herr Cardigan."

"Why?"

"So that in pursuing the truth, you'll stir things up and cause the current administration considerable grief. That in turn ought to provide me with material for a first rate exposé."

Jake studied the reporter's plump pink face, which had begun to perspire. "Tell me what you know about Beth Kittridge."

"What I suggest you had better do is contact a gentleman named Horst van Horn. He—"

"Wait now, Kreuz. Van Horn is the Director of the Berlin Forensic Medicine Center."

"Ja, exactly."

Jake said, "He headed the team that . . . that performed the autopsies on . . . on the victims. I . . ." Jake cleared his throat. "I read copies of his reports."

"Have a drink, please. It'll do you good, *mein herr.*"

"No, thanks." Jake rested an elbow on the table. "What about van Horn?"

"According to my sources, which I believe to be quite reliable, Doctor van Horn resorted to fakery in the case of the autopsy report dealing with Fräulein Kittridge."

"What do you mean?"

"I have, you must realize, no proof of this," explained the reporter. "Yet I am convinced that there is a strong possibility that the woman we saw coming to such a violent end was not Beth Kittridge at all."

Jake felt a sudden pain spread across his chest. Grimacing, he reached out and took hold of the other man's wrist. "They ran a DNA test on . . . on the remains. I saw the results," he told Kreuz, his voice no longer sounding exactly like his own. "There can't be any doubt that—"

"You're missing the point." The reporter pulled his arm free. "I have been informed that van Horn falsified his report. Don't you see?"

Jake sat back, feeling as though he'd just stopped running. Finally his breathing became regular and he said, "I'd better have a talk with van Horn."

"An excellent idea, *ja*," agreed Kreuz, smiling broadly.

The building Jake sought was around the corner from the New Reichstag. He reached the lobby of the Forensic Medicine Center a few minutes shy of five in the afternoon. The lobby was large, chill and grey.

One of the two black-enameled guardbots just inside the wide entry doors asked him, "Your business, *mein herr?*"

"I'd like to talk to Dr. van Horn."

"Quite impossible."

"Don't you want to know who I am before you toss me out?"

"It has nothing to do with who you are," rumbled the broadchested bot. "Dr. van Horn is much too busy to see anyone from the outside."

"Does he have a secretary?"

"Ja, of course."

"Might I talk to the secretary?"

Both robots let out impatient, exasperated sighs. "Follow Path 6," instructed one of them, "over to Desk 4."

Jake did that and found himself facing a silverplated, ball-headed robot. "I'd like to set up an appointment to talk with Dr. van Horn."

"Quite impossible."

"So I keep hearing," he said. "Look, my name is Jake Cardigan and I'm an operative with the Cosmos Detec—"

"Ja, that's all here." The robot was consulting one of the small greenish screens built into his metal desk top. "We also have a note to the effect that you have been causing trouble, Herr Cardigan, ever since you arrived in Berlin."

"On the contrary, I've been on my best—"

"You forced your way, for example, into a

detention center and contributed to the death of a prisoner."

"He was dying by the time I got there."

The silvery robot shook his head. "You have been advised to leave Berlin," he said. "Yet, quite obviously, you've ignored the—"

"I have to talk to van Horn. I'm trying to arrange this in a polite, legal and open way," said Jake evenly. "If I don't get to see him here, then I—"

"Are you threatening us, Herr Cardigan?"

Grinning thinly, he answered, "Nope, simply stating my position."

"You can not see the doctor," the robot told him. "If you refuse to leave at once, we'll summon secbots in sufficient numbers to eject you."

"Okay, I'll depart," said Jake, turning away. "But I'm going to talk to van Horn—eventually."

29

GOMEZ EMERGED FROM the bathroom of Jenny's minichalet, nodding. "That's the last room," he said as he dropped a small gadget into his jacket pocket. "No bugs or other eavesdropping equipment in any of your—"

"I told you already I swept the whole darn place with my own gear," the blonde agent said. She was standing by one of the parlor's leaded windows, looking out at the River Aare far below. "It's perfectly safe to talk here."

Out in the fading sky a Municipal Atmosphere skyvan flew by, spreading artificial snow over the city.

"I have the feeling our advent in Bern may've been anticipated." Gomez settled on the edge of her bed. "That's why I wanted to make doubly certain that nobody—"

"Worry about your own minichalet. When I say my rooms are safe, you can trust me that they are."

Gomez drummed his fingers on the bed. "According to the itinerary we got from the Amazing Otto, the Bonecas and their mechanical puppets will be showing up in the town of St. Norbert tomorrow afternoon," he said. "That's about an hour from here by landcar, so—"

"Yes, fine," she cut in. "You take care of renting us a car and we'll plan to leave here about two tomorrow afternoon."

"You seem restless and preoccupied, *chiquita.*"

"I haven't had a chance to unpack yet—and I like to take a nap after an air trip," she explained, still gazing out into the growing dusk. "Why don't you come back in . . . oh, about two hours, say, and we'll go to dinner. As long as we're stuck with each other, we may as well make the best of it."

Leaving the bed, the detective crossed to the door. "See you two hours hence."

Whistling softly, he walked out of her minichalet and along the flagstone path, which was dotted with newfallen snow, to his own minichalet next door.

"Better keep an eye on that *mujer,*" he advised himself. "If she slips away, it'll be a good idea to tag along."

He let himself into his shadowy parlor.

Gomez was walking toward the bedroom

when a faint humming began at the far side of the room.

Then the beam of a stungun hit him square in the chest.

As Jake entered his hotel suite, the vidphone started buzzing.

He ran over to the phone alcove. "Yeah?"

The screen remained blank. "Jake Cardigan?"

"That's me, yes." He sat facing the screen.

There was a silence that lasted ten seconds or more. *"Ja,* you appear to be Cardigan."

"I am, but who the hell are you?"

Very gradually an image formed on the screen. A greyhaired man of about fifty, with a neatly trimmed beard, was sitting in front of a blank grey wall. "I understand that you tried to obtain an interview with me earlier today," he said in his quiet, slightly nasal voice. "I regret that you were treated rudely. Yet you must understand that it wouldn't have been wise to—"

"Then you're Dr. van Horn?"

"Ja, and I desire to talk with you, Herr Cardigan."

Jake leaned forward. "Do you know something about Beth Kittridge?"

Van Horn nodded. "The autopsy report, which I understand you've read, was not exactly truthful."

"Is she . . . is Beth alive?"

"I regret that I was forced to . . ." He hesitated, then glanced nervously around. "I'm not certain how safe my vidphone is. Can you come to my home in an hour?" He gave Jake an address.

"Sure, but is she—"

"I can't talk any longer." The screen turned blank again.

The skycab set Jake down beside a small park near the Brandenburger Tor. At the center of the misty park a night concert was being held on an illuminated bandstand. The crimson-clad robot musicians, who were playing a brassy martial piece, seemed to be floating in the fog.

Somewhere, unseen, a small dog was yapping angrily.

Hands thrust down deep in his trouser pockets, Jake cut across the roadway.

Dr. van Horn's house had a high wrought-iron fence rising up in front of it. The gate was partially open.

Jake hurried up the path toward the front door of the narrow two-story townhouse.

The door swung silently open as he reached the top step of the porch. "Come in, please," invited the voice of the household computer.

Jake crossed the threshold and entered a softly illuminated hallway.

To his right the door of the living room slid open. "In here, if you please, Herr Cardigan."

The parlor was brightly lit by dozens of floating globes.

William Shatner

Sitting in a metallic chair, with a large bloody lazgun wound slashing across his chest, was the body of Dr. van Horn.

"Jake," said someone from the hall, "why did you kill this poor man?"

$\equiv$ 30 $\equiv$

THE SECOND TIME Dan glanced at the viewindow of his seaside living room, she was standing out there.

Slim and straight on the twilight beach. Molly grinned, waved and then pantomimed a request to be let into the condo.

He gave a resigned hunch of his shoulders, beckoning her to come around to the front door.

"Let this girl in," he told the front door.

"Very well, Danny."

"Hey, I'm not a kid. Call me Dan from now on."

"Very well, Dan."

The door whisked open and Molly entered. "Was that your house computer you were talking with?"

"Yep."

"It's sort of pretentious—a British accent."

"It happens not to be British, miss," the computer informed her. "But rather New England professorial."

"Pretentious, whatever the heck it is. Can you order it to keep still, Dan?"

"Don't interrupt for awhile," he said toward the nearest speaker outlet.

"I trust I know my place, sir."

Dan was studying the darkhaired young woman with his left eye narrowed. "Why exactly did you come over, Molly?"

"Have I ever told you how many guys at the academy are goofy in love with me?"

"No, and there's no need—"

"Over a dozen."

"I guess there might be at least a dozen loons at school. What's your point?"

"That you're darn lucky I honor you with my company." She sat on the sofa. "This thing is about as comfortable as a slab of neocrete."

"What do you want?"

"We're teamed up on a case, remember?"

"No, we aren't. *I'm* doing research on—"

"Do you know much about how avalanches work?"

"I understand the basic principle, yeah."

"Well, it'd be a good idea if you start thinking of me as an avalanche in your life," she advised him, grinning. "I'm inevitable and sooner or later I'm going to knock you clean off your feet."

"Ahum," said the computer.

"What?" asked Dan.

"Might we offer the young lady something in the way of refreshment?"

"No, but stand by to open the door when she leaves."

Laughing, Molly reached into a pocket of her skirt. "I came up with some material on Larry Knerr for you," she said, extracting a folded sheet of pale green paper.

"What is it?"

"Record of all the vidphone calls he made from his hotel while he was down in Rio de Janeiro."

"How the hell did you—"

"I'm persistent and persuasive," she explained, holding out the sheet of paper. "I can give you a quick summary of—"

"Yeah, all right, tell me who he called."

"That should be whom," she corrected. "Just because you're planning to be a lawman, there's no reason—"

"Tell me, Molly."

"Knerr made five calls to China Vargas. Two to her office at the *Fax-Times,* three to her home in the BevHills Sector."

Dan sat on the arm of a fat chair. "That's not especially surprising, since the guy works for her."

"And six calls to Roddy Pickfair."

"The boy genius who runs Ampersand Vid-pix?"

"That's the one. Pickfair is, by the way, only about four years older than you are."

"Knerr used to work for Ampersand," said Dan. "Is there anything odd about his calling the place?"

"Seems to me strange that a man who used to work for Bennett Sands would make so many calls to a company that was, until recently, controlled by Bennett Sands." She tapped the sheet on her bare knee. "Knerr got in touch with Pickfair more than he did with his boss."

"Maybe he and Pickfair are buddies."

Molly said, "Knerr also placed three calls to Lorenzo Mingus."

Dan stood up. "There are rumors that Mingus might be linked with the Tek trade."

"Mingus *is* linked."

"Which means Knerr could be linked, too," he said thoughtfully. "Or it could just be that Mingus is one of Knerr's news sources."

"Or they may have been exchanging beauty secrets. I doubt it, though." Rising, she returned the list to her pocket. "I noticed a passable seafood joint about a mile down the beach. Can we afford to dine there?"

"I suppose so, but—"

"Good. I like dinner meetings better than these at-home gatherings."

"We'll go to dinner, Molly," he said. "But

then you're going to head back to your dorm
and promise not to keep butting in. Okay?"

She asked, "Did you know, by the way, that
your condo is being watched?"

Inspector Spellman, a lazgun in his right hand,
came into the living room. "You should have
taken my advice and left town, Jake." He shook
his head sadly. He was carrying an opaque
plyosack in his left hand and he let it drop to
the floor. "Instead you remain in Berlin, behaving like a madman. You burst into the Forensic
Medicine Center, threaten poor Dr. van Horn.
Then you came here and killed him, apparently
because you had the crazed notion that he'd
lied about Beth Kittridge."

Grinning, Jake sat on another of the metal
armchairs. "Is the gun I used in that bag?"

"Ja, along with the Tek kit that'll be found
on your person."

"And I'm not going to be in any condition to
point out to anyone that this was all rigged by
you?"

"Nein, because you'll be dead, Jake. I'll have
to shoot you to keep you from attacking me."

Jake studied the policeman for a few silent
seconds. "How long have you been on the take,
Rhinehart?"

"Let's say rather that I'm subsidized by certain Tek interests," corrected the inspector.
"It's been nearly three years. My affiliation
began while you were away in the Freezer."

Jake said, "You knew in advance that they were going to kill Beth."

"Ah, you admit now that she's truly dead?" Spellman chuckled. "I thought perhaps we'd succeeded in convincing you she'd survived."

"I want to believe that, yeah," admitted Jake. "And when your man passed me that note, I did for awhile."

"But you don't now?"

"Not after the meeting with Kreuz."

"Wasn't the man convincing? I myself thought—"

"You were sloppy there, using a ringer instead of the real Kreuz." Jake shook his head. "Soon as I checked, I found out that the true Kreuz is in London on a story."

"That was a gamble."

Jake left the chair. "This whole thing has been for what? So you can kill me now?"

"You must keep in mind, my friend, that I don't plan these things," said Spellman. "For my tastes, this has all been much too cruel. But someone—well, someone higher up—wanted you toyed with for awhile before you were finally executed."

"And they're tired of toying?"

"Apparently."

"Well, I'll tell you," said Jake. "Your people pretty much foxed me in Brazil, got me close to believing I was going to find Will Sparey alive and well. But, shit—that won't work twice in a row."

Inspector Spellman frowned. "If you suspected a trap, why did you walk in here?"

"Because I wanted to see who'd spring the trap," he answered. "Now you're going to tell me who you're working for."

Spellman gestured with his lazgun. "Why should I do that?"

"Because I'm going to persuade you." Jake nodded toward the hall. "Come on in and lend me a hand," he called.

—=31=—

TIMECHECK, CARRYING A stunrifle, came into the deadman's living room. "I'll give you twenty-seven seconds to drop your weapon, Inspector," the overcoated Chinese told him.

"I had two men hidden outside," said the surprised policeman. "They should have stopped you from getting in here."

"I wouldn't hire them again were I you—they're not too efficient," said Timecheck. "You got twelve seconds left."

Spreading his fingers wide, Spellman let his lazgun fall. "I underestimated you, Jake," he said. "It was assumed you'd rush right over here as soon as our van Horn simulacrum contacted you. Instead you arranged for backup and—"

"Who are you working for?" Jake moved closer to him.

"You must realize that I can't tell you that."

"You haven't been paying close enough attention." Jake grabbed hold of the man's arms just above the elbows, shoved him back hard into the wall. "You helped kill Beth Kittridge. Now you're going to give me the names of the people involved in that, including your boss. If you don't—I'll simply kill you here and now and find out what I have to know from somebody else."

Spellman gave a thin, broken laugh. "You're a decent man, Jake," he said. "You don't slaughter people simply because—"

"I *used* to be a decent man," corrected Jake. "That was when you knew me in Greater LA years ago. Since then, though, the Teklords corrupted my wife, framed me and got me sent to the Freezer for four years. And now they killed the woman I was in love with." He rested his right hand on Spellman's throat. "I saw them kill her, saw her blown to pieces. Hell, everybody saw it—it was on television." His fingers tightened slightly. "Tell me what I want to know, or so help me god, I'll twist the life out of you."

The inspector made a gagging noise. "All right, I'll give you the names," he promised, gasping. "But, please, Jake, take your hand off me."

Jake increased the pressure. "Not quite yet," he said.

Birds had begun twittering, sunlight was making its way into Gomez's bedroom.

He awakened to find himself clad in a pair of purple pajamas and tucked neatly into his bed. "It's *mañana*," he realized, "but the last thing I recall is *noche*."

His head had that spongy feeling inside that follows being stungunned, and most of his bones, notably his spine, ached. With extreme care, he lifted the covers off himself and began the painful process of getting out of bed.

The birds continued singing in the sunny morning outside his minichalet. "Shut up, *por favor*," he requested in the direction of the nearest window.

His clothes and boots, which someone had thoughtfully removed from him, were arranged neatly beside his bed.

Gingerly, doing considerable wincing and cursing, Gomez got himself dressed.

At exactly 8 A.M. the voice of his chalet computer boomed out, "You left a wakeup call for eight A.M., Herr Gomez. It's time to arise."

"I've arisen." He glanced up at the ceiling speaker. "About what time did I leave that request?"

"The request was made at exactly 10:47 P.M. last evening and you sounded, if I may be so bold as to mention it, as though you'd recently returned from celebrating."

"That's me, a notorious bon vivant. Thanks."

Very quickly Gomez gathered up his belongings and dumped them all into his lone suitcase. His room had been deftly searched, but nothing had been taken.

Leaving the minichalet, he strolled over to Jenny's and tapped on the door.

After nearly a full minute the door opened halfway and a plump greyhaired woman in a flowered robe peered out. *"Ja?"*

Gomez smiled, bowing slightly. "I'm conducting a survey, *Frau,*" he informed her politely. "Is it safe to say you've never heard of Jenny Keaton?"

"Who?"

"And were I to ask you how long you've been residing in this particular chalet, your answer would be . . . ?"

"My husband and I have been here all this week," she answered. "Are you the fellow who had the loud party last night?"

"Quite probably." Bowing again, he went along the path to the central chalet of the hotel complex.

At the registration desk he tossed his electrokey to the clerkbot.

"Checking out, Herr Gomez?"

"With reluctance," he answered. "Would I be correct in assuming that you have no record of

a Miss Jenny Keaton having been registered
here?"

The robot touched a keypad, then looked at
one of the screens mounted on his desk. "That's
right."

Gomez nodded, got a fresh grip on his suitcase and took his leave.

He walked three blocks through the bright
morning city before he was satisfied nobody
was tailing him. Then he went into a landcar
rental office and picked up a vehicle.

When he reached the outskirts of Bern,
Gomez pulled into a parking lot beside a
sprawling restaurant with steeply slanting red
tile roofs. He slipped into one of the vidphone
booths that sat next to the place and made a
call to the Cosmos Detective Agency in Greater
Los Angeles.

Bascom himself answered. "You look frazzled," he observed.

"Contact your Internal Security chum," suggested Gomez. "Let him know that Jenny Keaton disappeared from her hotel in Bern, Switzerland, sometime between dusk last night and
dawn this morning."

"Who's responsible?"

"No idea, *jefe*," replied Gomez, shrugging.
"Could be the lass was snatched by members of
the opposition or she might have arranged her
vanishing herself. The residents and the man-
agement are pretending she was never there at

all and I don't have the time or temperament to play that kind of game."

"What are you planning to do?"

"I'm heading for the town of St. Norbert to see if I can catch up with the Boneca bunch."

Bascom eyed him. "And you don't feel obliged to linger in Bern to lead the search for the missing damsel?"

"Somebody stungunned me at sunset last night," he explained. "It's just possible that the missing damsel arranged that. But whatever the case may be, I don't intend to schlep around Bern devoting myself to the problem."

"You're not as sentimental as you used to be," said his chief.

"That's very true," agreed Gomez. He hung up and hurried back to his landcar.

═ 32 ═

TIMECHECK ROLLED UP the sleeve of his overcoat to consult his arm. "Your Maglev Express for Vienna will be departing in eight minutes and twenty-two seconds," he told Jake, nodding at the sleek silvery passenger car that stood next to the underground platform. "That is if it sticks to its 9:13 A.M. departure time."

"You didn't have to see me off."

"I want, hey, to impress you with my versatility," explained the Chinese. "You have long known me as a dependable source of info. Last night, though, after I served in that tried and true capacity, I helped you get the drop on Assistant Inspector Spellman."

"And I appreciate your helping out in that emergency."

"Today I'm here to see you get your butt safely clear of Berlin," he said. "I hope you didn't mind my scramming last night before the cops arrived."

"Nope, not at all."

"Everything turned out okay, didn't it?"

Jake said, "Yeah, Spellman decided to confess his Tek affiliation to Inspector Hauser when he arrived. Though he didn't give him the names he gave me—not yet. Spellman is in custody—and I'm free to go to Vienna to hunt down the people he says he was working for. I should beat the cops to them."

"You better be damn careful," cautioned Timecheck. "It's near certain that some of those guys are going to be expecting you."

"I'm prepared for that."

He looked at his arm again. "Three minutes and forty-six seconds left," Timecheck announced. "You better hop on board."

Jake picked up his suitcase. "Thanks again."

"You put on a terrific act last night, you know. I was impressed," he told Jake. "When you told Spellman you'd kill him if he didn't talk, that sounded convincing as hell."

"I'm not certain I *was* acting." Jake stepped aboard the train.

By the time he reached the little mountain town of St. Norbert, Gomez's head was no longer full of fuzz. Nearly all the aftereffects of having been knocked unconscious by a stungun the night before had faded, too, except for a mild pain that worked its way up and down his spine now and then.

He parked his rented landcar at a lot near the town square. After charging the parking on his Banx card, he inquired of the robot attendant, "How do I get to the Electro Theatre?"

"That's quite simple," answered the mechanical man, pointing downhill. "You walk along this lane until you come to the Blume Fountain, then go left for three blocks. That will put you at the Abendmal Fountain. You go down the alleyway to the right for five blocks, cross Soldat Square and turn into Schlummer Road. You'll find the Electro at the end of that."

"Much obliged, *gracias.*"

The midmorning air was crisp and clear. Rising up all around the town were the white-capped peaks of the Bernese Alps.

"Impressive," decided the detective as he strode along the imitation cobblestones of the roadway.

He caught up with a party of ten middleaged tourists who were being escorted through the town by a white-enameled robot guide wearing a bright Tyrolean hat.

Gomez skirted the group, passed them and walked on briskly to the fountain. At its center rose a metallic obelisk some thirty feet high. Hundreds of glittering multicolored metal flowers were twined around the column, and in the pool at its base dozens of real fish flashed in the pale blue water.

Turning left, Gomez started walking rapidly toward his next landmark.

When he passed a narrow cafe, the mingled scents of cocoa and cinnamon pastries caused him to slow his pace and recall that he hadn't as yet had breakfast.

A plump android in a white suit and high chef's hat waved at him from the doorway, beckoning him in.

"Business first," called Gomez, continuing on his way.

About a block beyond the next fountain, he began to suspect he was no longer heading in the right direction. At the corner he spotted a uniformed robot patrolman.

"I'm seeking the Electro Theatre," he told the mechanical cop.

"Oh, *ja,*" said the robot. "That used to be only a few short blocks from here."

Gomez blinked. "Used to be?"

"It blew up."

"When did that occur?"

The robot consulted his watch. "Approximately two and a half hours ago," he replied.

=33=

ON THE VIDWALL screen the Electro Theatre exploded again, sending fire, thick sooty smoke and great jagged chunks of metal and plastiglass erupting up into the clear morning.

"Hold it there." Gomez stepped up closer to the wall and pointed at the lower righthand corner of the screen. "This is the person I was alluding to."

"*Ja*, of course," said Sergeant Dibble of the St. Norbert Town Police. "I didn't notice her on the prior viewing."

"She seems to be wearing some sort of religious outfit."

"Moritz, what is her name again?" the sergeant inquired of the robot officer who was seated at one of the small office's two desks.

"Sister Jonquil. The dear young lady had been calling at the theater, collecting for charity, just prior to the explosion."

The vidwall picture continued. "Looks like the force of the explosion knocks her over," said Gomez.

"Most unfortunate." The chubby sergeant tugged at a corner of his bristly moustache. "She was quite shaken up."

"Seriously injured?"

"We're anticipating that she was not, Herr Gomez. But she is at the Wayfarer's Hospital just now for observation—Moritz, be sure to phone later to ask about Sister Jonquil's condition."

"I intended to."

The film ended and Gomez asked, "This footage, you said, was taken by your monitor camera system?"

"We have robocams that circulate through the town, feeding pictures back here to our central monitor screens. That way we keep track of what's going on all across St. Norbert."

"This snippet you've so kindly screened for me," mentioned the detective, "is not especially lengthy. It doesn't show anyone entering the theater, not even Sister Jonquil."

Nodding ruefully, the sergeant replied, "Because of our last budget cuts we can't keep the cameras running all the time."

Gomez leaned against the wall. "Have you determined what caused the explosion?"

"Not yet," answered Dibble. "We're certain it wasn't an accident."

"What about the Bonecas?"

"Alas," sighed Moritz.

"Dead?"

Dibble said, "We found the remains of two people, a man and a woman, in the ruins of the theater, along with the remains of some twenty five or so mechanical puppets. It hasn't yet been determined if the bodies are those of Boneca and his wife."

"They aren't anywhere else," reminded Moritz.

"True. The puppeteers left their hotel, apparently headed for the theater, a good hour prior to the explosion. There is no trace of them anywhere in town."

"Where's the Wayfarer's Hospital located?"

After giving him directions, the police sergeant asked, "Why is the prestigious Cosmos Detective Agency interested in this pair of wandering players?"

"It's a routine insurance matter," Gomez lied. Smiling at them, he eased toward the door.

Gomez frowned over the top of the bunch of yellow plazroses he was carrying. "Are you sure, doctor?"

The handsome blond android physician nodded. "We advised her to remain here longer," he said, "but she insisted on signing herself out. She had to get back to her convent at once."

The lobby of the Wayfarer's Hospital was walled with plastiglass and afforded a sweeping view of Alpine peaks.

Gomez let his bouquet swing down to his side. "I don't suppose Sister Jonquil mentioned which convent she was affiliated with?"

The android medic said, "You know, she didn't."

"What did she leave in—landcab or skycab?"

"As a matter of fact, she persuaded one of our robot interns to fetch her own landcar, which she'd left at her hotel parking lot."

"Do you know where she headed from here?"

"Downhill is all I saw," said the doctor. "You seem, *mein herr,* most eager to find her."

"I feel a sudden need for religious guidance," explained Gomez, handing him the flowers. "Give these to somebody who doesn't have any."

"Why, thank you. You intend to try to find her?"

"I plan to, yes."

"It'll be next to impossible, won't it?"

"It'll be," said Gomez, "challenging."

Ten of the robot dogs started barking when Gomez entered the shop.

"Quiet, you fiends!" cried the proprietor of SnoHounds, Ltd. "Stop that nervewracking din!"

"I'm in search of Helmut Kolb, Jr.," shouted the detective.

The proprietor, a lean, balding man in his fifties, came out from behind his desk. "They're not supposed to bark like this," he said apologetically. "Silence!"

There were fifteen mechanical dogs, most of them St. Bernard size, in the small showroom. Each chromeplated mechanical animal occupied its own pedestal. Seven of the largest continued to bark in deep tinny voices.

"Is Helmut Kolb, Jr., hereabouts?" asked Gomez loudly.

"Just a moment, *mein herr.*" The owner yanked out a stungun.

Gomez pulled his stungun as well. "If you're contemplating—"

"Nein, nein, relax. I merely use this to control those idiotic tin hounds," he explained. "Look, you devils! You see this gun? Stop your yowling at once!"

All but one of the robot dogs turned silent.

A huge glistening one, glaring directly at Gomez, kept on gruffing loudly.

"I warned you!" The proprietor fired.

The beam hit the big mechanical dog in the chest. He ceased barking, his mouth snapping shut with a clang. Then, after taking three wobbly steps backwards on his display pedestal, he teetered and fell. He smacked the showroom floor with an echoing thunk.

"No wonder business has been so rotten."

The owner holstered his gun. "Nobody wants to rent a mountain guide dog who is so rowdy and illmannered."

Glancing from the fallen SnoHound to the balding man, Gomez said, "I was told I could contact Helmut Kolb, Jr., here."

"What a mistake that was."

"Which?"

"Naming that lazy lummox after myself." Returning to his desk, he perched on its edge. "Makes it much more difficult to deny he's mine."

"Is he here?"

"What did you want with him?"

"An informant of mine suggested—"

"Never mind, it would probably break my poor old heart to learn what sort of new mischief he's up to," said Helmut Kolb, Sr. "Although, I must say, you don't appear to be as seedy and disreputable as the usual lowlifes who come here to consult my boy."

"*Gracias*. Where is he?"

The owner pointed at a green door behind him. "Through there."

"Much obliged."

"I don't suppose you'd be interested in hiring a SnoHound? I can give you a terrific discount."

"I won't have time for any mountain climbing this trip." Gomez crossed to the door. "Otherwise I'd be tempted."

"I didn't think you'd want one. Nobody does."

Gomez went through the doorway, along a narrow corridor and into a small square room jammed with electronic equipment, computer terminals and several animated pinup paintings.

Helmut Kolb, Jr., was a fat young man of thirty, wearing a flowered shirt and white trousers. He sat in a slingchair, scowling at the eclair he was holding in his left hand. "You're Gomez, right?"

"I am."

"I was told you'd drop by. Smell this." He held out the eclair.

Gomez obligingly took a sniff. "And now?"

"Smells stale to me."

Gomez settled into a chair. "I was told you're the only gent in town who—"

"It doesn't smell stale to you?"

"Not in the least. What I want is—"

"I'll risk it then." The younger Kolb took a substantial bite. "Tastes stale." He set it atop a databox. "My fee is $500."

"The rate I heard was—"

"But you didn't hear that from me."

"$400."

"$475."

"$450."

"Done. What do you want to know?"

"I'm interested in the peregrinations of a young lady who left St. Norbert a few hours ago in a rented landcar." Gomez provided the fat young man with a description of Jenny Keaton and her car. "She's been using the name Sister Jonquil of late, but I imagine she'll have shed it by now."

"Even stale that wasn't so bad." Helmut had picked up the eclair and finished it. He then put on a pair of opaque goggles that were equipped with massive earphones.

After roughly sixty seconds one of the screens on the far wall started blinking a bright red. A simulated photo of Jenny, dressed in a simple grey skirtsuit, appeared on the screen.

"That is she, *sí.*"

Removing the goggles and earphones, Helmut touched a keyboard at his left.

From a speaker dangling near Gomez's left ear came a hollow rasping voice. "This woman, calling herself Jillian Kearny, left the Bern skyport seventeen minutes ago."

"Bound for where?"

Out in the showroom nine of the robot dogs started barking loudly.

"The destination of her skyliner is Vienna, Austria."

The barking increased in intensity.

Helmut Kolb, Sr., yelled, "Look out! They . . ."

=34=

Jake's landcab let him out near the Schwar-
zenbergplatz. It was a clear windy day in
Vienna and most of the tables at the outdoor
cafe across the way were unoccupied. A highly-
polished silver waiterbot stood idly in the doorway and from inside the place amplified zither
music was drifting.

Crossing the street, he went through the narrow doorway of the three-story brick building
next to the cafe. Jake climbed the staircase to
the second floor, walked along the corridor to
the door labeled JOHAN GEWITTER, ACCOUNTANT.

A scancam over the door looked him over. A
mechanical voice greeted, "Welcome, *mein
herr.*" The metal door clicked, swung open.

Jake entered the office. "You're Gewitter?"

A handsome blond man of about forty sat behind the white desk, smiling at Jake from the far side of the white office. "I'm not here right now," he said cordially, "but this first-rate android simulacrum will be happy to take care of your any need."

Moving a few steps closer to the sim, Jake asked, "When will you be back?"

The android inquired, "You're Jake Cardigan?"

"Yeah."

"Sit down, Herr Cardigan," he invited, pointing at a stiff white chair. "Timecheck phoned to tell us you'd be dropping in. I'm not here, but Sonny Boy is more than capable of handling your problem."

"You're Sonny Boy?" He frowned at the android and remained standing.

"His idea, not mine. Sit, please," said the simulacrum. "Actually I'm smarter than Herr Gewitter—and I don't have an ulcer."

"Even so, I'd prefer—"

"He's out of town," explained the android. "An accounting job for a bunch of swindlers in Salzburg."

"I can't wait."

"Let me assure you that I'm equipped to handle this." He held up his right hand. "Besides which, I've been especially designed to interface with all this first-rate equipment." He gestured at the computer terminals and info-screens built into two of the white walls.

Jake sat, tentatively, in the stiff white chair. "I have to contact—and question—a gent named D. E. Nister," he said, mentioning the name he'd persuaded Inspector Spellman to pass along. "He's a professor of Technobiology at the Austrian Academic Network."

"And also connected with the largest Tek cartel in Europe." The Gewitter android tapped a sheaf of papers atop the desk. "I did some backgrounding soon as Timecheck contacted me."

"From what I learned in Berlin, I suspected as much." Jake leaned forward. "By now it's possible that Professor Nister suspects I'm interested in him. I need a reliable informant, which Timecheck assured me you are, to help me find out where the prof might hole up."

"That's a challenging problem," said the android. "Nister doesn't broadcast from the regular AAN studios. In addition, his lectures for the past two days have been repeats."

"Where do they originate?"

"From a private studio in his home near the Riesenrad."

"But he's not at home?"

Tapping the report, the sim answered, "Not according to my sources."

"Then we have to find out where he is."

"Exactly, *mein herr.*" The android left his chair to walk to the nearest wall. "Earlier I sent out some discreet queries." He inserted his forefinger into a socket beneath one of the infoscreens. "Any news that's come in during the past few minutes will automatically be transferred from here to my brain. Then I can tell you what—"

"Wouldn't it be simpler for me just to read it off—"

"Nein, this particular capacity cost a great deal. Not to make use of it would . . . *Gott!"*

Suddenly the screen turned bright red. The socket crackled and sputtered, the android's hand began to glow and throw off an impressive shower of gold and yellow sparks. His entire body stiffened as he rose up on his toes and commenced howling.

His eyeballs melted and went splashing down his cheeks. His blond hair stood straight up and then burned swiftly away to soot. He was flung back from the wall.

The burned-out android fell back onto his desk, dropped to the floor and lay on his side, twitching and kicking.

His mouth snapped open and he started spewing out twists of bright-colored wire, tiny coppery cogs and steaming spurts of greenish oil.

Jake grabbed the report up off the desk and thrust it into a pocket. Pivoting, he ran to the door and into the hall. "Looks like it's going to be tougher than I thought to arrange a chat with the professor," he reflected as he hurried for the stairs.

* * *

The Neptune Cafe was built out over the Pacific Ocean and the night surf hit low at its tinted plastiglass walls. Dan had left Molly in a booth in the central dining area and made his way to a vidphone booth.

He called the offices of the Cosmos Detective Agency. When a robot showed on the screen, Jake's son said, "I want to leave a message for Walt Bascom. Ask him if—"

"Don't be shy, lad." Bascom appeared on the phonescreen. "Ask me directly."

Dan asked, "Do you have somebody watching me?"

"What makes you ask?"

"Do you? Because if you don't, then somebody—"

"Describe this alleged tail."

"Well, actually I haven't seen him myself. But a friend of mine—not a friend exactly, somebody from the academy, a fellow student— spotted him near the condo, keeping an eye on the place," explained Dan. "A slim man, about thirty, shortcropped blond hair. He one of yours?"

"Yep, that's McCay," admitted Bascom. "Who's the young lady who noticed him?"

"Oh, Molly Fine. Basically she's a nuisance."

"But perceptive."

"I suppose so. Why do you—"

"Your father's concerned, Dan. So am I. That's why I have operatives—"

"If it's all the same to you, I can take care of

myself," Dan assured him. "So you can retire
McCay and whoever else you assigned to baby-
sit."

"It'd be smarter to keep—"

"Isn't necessary."

"Very well." Bascom nodded amiably. "From
now on you're on your own. Okay?"

"Thanks, yeah."

Back at the booth Dan said, "It *was* one of
the Cosmos operatives. Sort of a nursemaid
that my dad thought I needed."

"And?" asked Molly.

"Bascom's calling him off," he said. "He also
suggested that we quit playing detective."

"How'd he find out about that?"

"He's a detective, too," reminded Dan. "Anyway, I think I will give this up. Too dangerous
and I ought to be concentrating on my academy
work. So from now on, Molly, I won't be need-
ing your help."

Molly smiled. "Neither you or Bascom are
especially good liars," she pointed out. "He's
not going to call off the surveillance—and you
aren't really planning to quit investigating
Knerr." Her smile widened. "You'll have to do
better than this if you want to ditch me."

—≡ 35 ≡—

THE FIRST ONE who came charging into the back room of the SnoHound shop was a chrome-plated robot wearing a knitcap and a crimson parka. He held a lazgun in each gloved hand.

Gomez was ducked behind a clutter of Helmut Kolb, Jr.'s, gadgets. Helmut, a considerable portion of him still visible, was crouched to the rear of a stack of databoxes.

The robot spotted him, aimed twin guns at his backside as he ordered, "On your feet, fatass."

Gomez popped up, firing his stungun at the intruding robot.

The beam proved sufficient to disable the mechanical man and he tumbled over into the chair Helmut had recently occupied.

A booted foot stepped across the threshold and Gomez kicked out at it.

Someone yelled, then a bald youth in a black jacket came stumbling in.

Gomez fired his stungun again. Scooping up the unconscious youth, he used him as a shield and went rushing out into the showroom.

He tripped over the sprawled proprietor, let go of the bald young man just as the other two intruders fired their lazguns in his direction.

The youth was sliced in half and then in quarters, but by that time Gomez was sheltered behind the metal counter.

He scuttled along the floor, reached one of the barking robot dogs on its pedestal. Swiftly he punched out instructions on the hound's control panel. "Sic 'em," he ordered.

Growling ferociously, the big metallic dog leaped from his pedestal and straight at the bearded man who was in the act of swinging his ebony lazgun toward the scurrying Gomez.

The hound hit the big man full in the chest with both metal forepaws, knocking him off balance. The lazgun crackled, digging a deep zigzag rut in the ceiling.

The final intruder was a copperplated robot who stood near the door to the street.

By the time the bearded gunman hit the floor, Gomez had successfully programmed two more of the SnoHounds to go into action.

They both charged the robot, knocking him

to the floor before he could get his gun trained on the dodging detective.

Gomez bounded across the floor, kneeled next to the fallen bot and fired his stungun at him.

Then, retrieving the bearded man's dropped lazgun, he squatted beside him. The robot hound was still holding him down with his metal paws.

"Okay, *hombre,* who sent you?"

All the other robot hounds were barking enthusiastically and the bearded man asked, "What did you say, asshole?"

Gomez shouted, "Who hired you?"

"Up your gazoo, greaseball."

Gomez jabbed the barrel of the lazgun into the downed man's side. "Here's how I see your immediate future, *cabrón,*" he told him. "After you get out of the hospital, you'll—"

"Bullshit, you won't use that lazgun on me. You're a cop and your code of—"

"Por favor, allow me to conclude my dire prediction," requested Gomez, shoving the gun deeper into his side. "You'll be heading for the hospital not because of me, but because this enormous *perro* is going to chomp some extremely essential parts of your anatomy. I can program him to—"

At that point another of the dogs jumped from his perch, galloped over and sank his teeth into Gomez's thigh.

He gave a yell of pain, distracted.

The bearded man took advantage of that, kicking him in the midsection and then rolling free of the other robot dog. He ran for the door, pushed his way out into the street.

Twisting, Gomez used his own stungun again and managed to disable the dog that was chomping on him. "You picked a dandy time to go berserk," he told the now immobile robot.

"They're all like that. You can't trust a damned one of them." Helmut Kolb, Sr., was sitting up, touching carefully at the bloody lump on his forehead. "Who did these hoodlums come here to rough up—you or my worthless son?"

"Me." Gomez got shakily to his feet. "I'll turn the remains over to the law, but the only human left who can talk is the one who scooted away while Fido here was sinking his tusks into me."

Accepting Gomez's assistance in rising off the floor, the senior Kolb asked, "Are you planning to visit us regularly, *mein herr?*"

"If all goes well," Gomez assured him, "neither you nor Switzerland will ever see the likes of me again."

═ 36 ═

GOMEZ GAVE A hobbling jump to one side as a thickset man with a spiky red beard came stumbling backwards across the main concourse of the Vienna Skyport toward him.

The man missed colliding with him and went tottering by, tripped over somebody else's sitting suitcase and fell on his backside with a smacking thump.

A husky blonde woman of forty ran up, dealt the fallen man a disabling chop to the neck. She clamped a set of electrocuffs on him, gave a satisfied nod and walked over to Gomez. "How come you're so gimpy, Sid?" she inquired as she held out her hand.

"I was recently bitten by a robot," he explained, shaking hands. "Why'd you toss that *hombre*, Eva?"

"The walleyed sap tried to snatch my purse," explained Eva Kraft, waving at the robot security cop who was hurrying over. "Another one for you, Hans."

The chromeplated robot tipped his police cap, gave an appreciative chuckle and gathered up the pursesnatcher. *"Wunderbar,"* he commented.

Gomez rested his suitcase and coughed into his hand. "You are, as you know, one of my favorite private operatives in all the world," he assured the husky blonde woman, "and the Cosmos Detective Agency has long relied on—"

"Don't go acting like a gaptoothed ninny, Sid," she advised him. "Come right out and say that I embarrass you."

"It's only that I was hoping, *chiquita,* to make an unobtrusive entrance into your fair city." He picked up his suitcase. "Having enormous louts flung at my feet, I've found, tends to attract attention."

"It couldn't be helped," the detective told him. "I was standing there, blending artfully in with the hundreds of ninnies and simps who clutter up the skyport when that crosseyed sappo made a try for my—"

"I appreciate your coming down to meet me." He started to limp toward an exit ramp. "Have you found out anything about the activities of Jenny Keaton?"

"I started work on the project soon as you

phoned from that dinky tourist trap in Switzerland."

"And what have you—"

"I picked up the little ninny's trail. It wasn't
all that difficult," said Eva. "She checked into
the Hotel Freundlich on the Augustinerstrasse.
She's currently using the moniker Jolline
Kurtzman."

"Bueno. Let's get over there."

"That won't do you any good, *liebling."* They
stepped out onto a skycar parking lot. The day
was fading and a sharp wind blew across the
dusky area.

"Why not, Evita?"

"Because your friend Jenny—my car's the
purple one over there—left her hotel after only
fifteen minutes and took a landcab to the Dings
Flohmarkt near the Kettenbrückengasse Maglev Station. That's a—"

"Gadget fleamarket. And?"

Eva slowed, scowling. "Well, then something
odd took place, Sid," she replied, sounding
both annoyed and perplexed. "The lady flung a
wingding."

"Be a mite more specific."

"She went bonkers, had a fit, acted in a
highly irrational manner. She ended up being
hauled off by the medics."

Gomez halted, asking, "Where is she now?"

"They took the poor woman to the Berggasse
Foundation, which is a privately owned loony
bin, for observation," said the investigator. "I

have some connections, so we may be able to spring her from—"

"Nix. A little observation will do Jenny good. We'll get around to her later," said Gomez. "What I want to do, *muy pronto,* is get to that fleamarket. We have to find out whom she was trying to contact there."

Very quietly Jake lowered the butler to the floor. The android made a faint thumping noise as Jake arranged him on the thick carpeting of the corridor.

Standing up and away, he glanced down the shadowy hallway. His stungun was held in his right hand. Nodding to himself, he continued deeper into the townhouse. After turning a bend in the hall, he saw a large rectangle of light up ahead on his left.

It was the open doorway of the studio he sought. Jake slowed his pace, listening. Except for the soft hums and purrs of its various mechanisms, the house was quiet.

Jake eased closer to the studio. He became aware now of footfalls on a bare wooden floor and then a chair scraping in there. Halting just short of the doorway, he brought his gun up to chest level.

After listening for another full minute, he stepped carefully into the brightly lighted room. "Good evening, Fräulein Roth," he said.

The slender blonde woman didn't flinch. She simply pushed her chair back from the keyboard she'd been working at and turned to look him over. "You must be Jake Cardigan," said Mina Roth. "I've seen photographs of you."

"I imagine you have." He was watching her very carefully.

She left her chair, crossing to a large vidscreen on the wall. It showed the glittering unfinished landscape painting she was at work on. "I have a quite expensive security system." She leaned back against the wall, studying him.

"I have considerable experience in circumventing security systems," he told her. "And in incapacitating robots, androids and assorted servos."

"Is there, Herr Cardigan, any special reason why you've so rudely intruded into my home?"

He moved closer to the artist. "Earlier today, before he was destroyed, a Johan Gewitter android compiled a report for me on the activities, professional and otherwise, of Professor D. E. Nister."

She smiled faintly. "Was this late mechanism a scandal columnist, a private investigator or—"

"A supplier of information, stuff he gathered in unorthodox ways," said Jake. "We're going to talk about Nister now."

"He's not here. I have no idea where he is," she assured him. "You've invaded my privacy for nothing, Herr Cardigan."

"You happen to be the professor's current

mistress, Fräulein Roth. I want you to tell me where the guy is."

"Why not contact the real Gewitter, wherever he may be, and see if he can help you out?"

"He's decided to drop from sight." Jake grinned bleakly at her. "You're the most likely source of information."

Mina Roth returned to her chair, sat, rested her right hand on the keyboard. "Nister never comes here," she said. "He hasn't contacted me in several days." She touched a few keys and a cloud was added to the landscape painting. "I do hope that you didn't pay very much for your information, since it's far from accurate."

"Actually, I didn't pay a damn thing for it. They fried the andy before—"

"Enough!" She'd popped the keyboard open and snatched out a lazgun from a compartment within.

As she spun to fire at him, Jake threw himself to the right.

He squeezed the trigger of his stungun as he fell. The beam hit her just below her left breast.

The blonde gasped, bit her lower lip. Her arms and legs went rigid, her eyes snapped shut.

In falling, she smashed into the keyboard. That modified the painting, causing explosions of scarlet light to appear among the pine trees.

"Damn," said Jake, walking over and collecting her gun out of her stiffened fingers. "I wanted to question her."

William Shatner

As he tucked the weapon into his jacket
pocket, he scanned the large room. There was a
vidphone sitting in an alcove near the doorway.

Jake sat down at the phone. "Let's see," he
said, "what you can tell me."

══37══

THE DINGS FLOHMARKT consisted of a 5-story-high atrium ringed with wide balconies that were trimmed with fat chrome railings and hundreds of plastiglass lightbubbles. The ground level was given over to vendors of math gadgets, nearly fifty of them hawking from booths, kiosks, tables and stools.

"Mathats! Mathats!" cried a thin black man who was perched on a rickety tin stool and holding a chromed derby aloft. "Place it on your coco and in just seconds you'll be doing algebra or . . ."

"Smallest calculator known to man!" offered a plump woman who was wearing a polka dot scarf. "Size of a flyspeck."

"Out of the way, you lopeared ninny," suggested Eva, giving the zealous vendor a shove that cleared her from their path. "Your chum was up on Level 2, Gomez, when she flung her wingding."

"Where exactly?"

"Hey, you elephantine bimbo, you knocked six of my calculators out of my mitt with that brutal and uncalled for shove." The woman was on hands and knees, patting wildly at the floor. "Finding six of the tiniest calculators in the world is no easy task. Why not simply pay me the $50 each that they're worth and we'll call—"

"Don't be a walleyed simp. I don't owe you a damn thing." Eva halted and glared down at the woman. "Jenny was near the mechanical doll sellers, Gomez, when—"

"How about you pay for just three of my flyspeck calculators and I'll absorb the cost of—"

"How about I detach your nose from your pudding face?"

"I'll trot on up to Level 2, Eva," said Gomez. "Join me when you're finished with this fracas."

"It'll only take a moment or two." The husky detective started to roll up her sleeves. "Now, let's . . ."

Gomez hurried up the ramp to the next level. He came first to the sellers of household gadgets.

"Talking vacuum cleaners," offered a shaggy man in a small lopsided booth. "The perfect

218

companion for a lonely bachelor such as yourself, sir."

"I'm happily wed," Gomez assured him, continuing along.

"Pocket icecube maker! No one should be
without this handy device. How about you,
sir?"

"You're absolutely right. And I happen to
have one in my pocket already."

There were about thirty dealers in mechanical dolls and robot toys. At a large table on
Gomez's right a dozen identical 2-foot-high
blonde little girl dolls were tapdancing in uni-
son. As he passed the table, one of the curly-
headed dolls danced right off the edge and fell
to the floor.

Bending, he retrieved it. "Talk to your chore-
ographer, *chiquita*," he advised. "You're . . .
ow!"

Something jagged beneath the doll's frilly
skirt had scratched at his hand. He set the doll
back on the counter, fished out a plyochief and
dabbed at the small bleeding scratch and then
moved on.

He hadn't noticed before that the next vendor was trying to unload SnoHounds. Six of
them sat on the floor surrounding the plump
man.

"What a treat," exclaimed one of the dogs,
"encountering you once again, Herr Gomez."

He stopped, frowning. "I didn't know you
guys could talk."

"Talk and sing," another assured him. "Also tapdance."

"And do math."

"Well, nice meeting you." Gomez took his leave.

The next fleamarketeer had a counter covered with foot-high dolls that were modeled after Jenny Keaton.

"Now this *hombre* must know something," said Gomez aloud.

"What's the matter, *mein herr?*"

"I'm trying to locate the *mujer* who posed for these," he explained, noticing that the dolls had grown larger.

"Why don't you simply ask me, Gomez?" inquired one of the dolls. "Can't you do a darn thing right?"

"Why not indeed." He picked it up, brought it close to his face. "Where have you gotten to?"

"Mein herr, please, put that down. You're liable to break it."

"But this is a friend and associate of mine, so it's perfectly okay . . . Anyway, grizzly bears aren't allowed to conduct business in Austria. They can waltz, that's perfectly all right, but—"

"I must insist," growled the huge bear, who was coming around from behind the counter.

Gomez ducked, got in under the swinging paws and started punching the bear's furry midsection. "It's okay, folks," he shouted, "I'll take care of this critter. No need to panic."

"Another crazy person," cried the bear. "Help!"

"Better summon the market patrol again."

"I'll fetch them. *Ach,* such a day we're having!"

As he struggled with the shaggy bear, Gomez thought, *"Deus,* is it possible that *I'm* flinging a wingding?"

Then someone used a stungun on him.

Dan scanned the front page of the morning *GLA Fax-Times* as it came rolling out of the wallslot. Before the second page was completely printed, he was dressed and leaving the apartment.

Rex/GK-30 groaned and lurched up out of his wicker rocker when the young man came hurrying into the Background & ID room. "Geeze, what a day this is shaping up to be," he complained. "Now what?"

Waving the fresh front page at the robot, Dan said, "There's a charity dance tonight at the Greater LA Civic Plaza in the Westwood Sector—to raise money for the Veterans of the Brazil Wars Fund."

"So I've heard." He sat again.

"It says that Larry Knerr *and* Roddy Pickfair will be there. As well as China Vargas."

"Along with a thousand other prominent citizens of GLA."

"Exactly," said Dan, "and some of them will be my age. A few anyway, so I won't stand out."

Rex eyed him. "Let me see, kiddo, if I can hazard a guess as to what you have in mind," he said as he rocked slowly in his chair. "You're figuring to attend this shindig and mingle with the crush. You'll keep an eye out for Knerr and if he gets into a conversation with anyone interesting, such as Roddy Pickfair, you'll do a little eavesdropping. Maybe you'll do it from a safe distance, using some sort of compact electronic listening device."

"Yeah, I'll borrow one of my dad's. It's no bigger than . . . Hey, how come you guessed all this?"

"Guessing the obvious doesn't take one heck of a lot of brains." The robot tapped his metal skull with a coppery finger.

"You could arrange everything easy, Rex, with all that you have access to," Dan told him. "Get my name added to the guest list, print up a fake invitation that'll be good enough to fool them. Can you? Will you?"

"What is the purpose of all this tomfoolery?"

"I want to help my dad, you know that. I'm certain that Larry Knerr is involved with what happened in Brazil—and probably in Beth's murder."

Rex asked him, "Just *one* invite?"

"Sure, for me," answered Dan. "I don't intend to drag Molly along to something like this. She'd simply futz up my investigation."

"Molly, bless her, is far more generous and thoughtful than you." The big robot picked a square of cream-colored paper off the top of a packing case. "She had me run off *two* of these buggers. One for her *and* one for you."

"Molly," he said. "She's already been here?"

"At the crack of dawn," replied the robot. "She took her invite along with her and says you're to pick her up at her dorm *promptly* at 8:30 tonight." He held out Dan's invitation toward him.

"If I don't take her, she'll go anyway."

"Without a doubt, kiddo."

"I'll take her." He accepted the invitation.

=38=

"I'M DARNED DISAPPOINTED in you."

Gomez groaned, but didn't open his eyes.

"Brains I wasn't expecting, though I was sort of hoping you might use simple brute force to bust me out of here."

Gomez groaned again. He was lying on something cold and hard, probably a floor. Gingerly, he felt at it. Yes, definitely a floor, a metal one.

"Instead, you let them snare you, the same as they did me. So now we're both stuck."

He opened his eyes tentatively, saw Jenny Keaton crouched beside him in the small grey room. Groaning once more, he shut his eyes.

"This is no time to play possum." She poked him in the side with her forefinger.

"Twice," he muttered in a somewhat rusty voice.

224

"Whatever are you babbling about?" asked the Internal Security agent.

Unaided, he sat up. "Twice in the short time since I've met you, *chiquita,* have I been felled by a stungun."

"Well, I had nothing to do with it this time."

"That's a comfort." Reaching out, he pressed his palm against the grey metal wall. "You *are* taking credit, I notice, for my being zapped in picturesque Bern, Switzerland."

"I hired a local operative to handle that." She stood back out of his way as he began the slow, wobbly process of rising to his feet. "That was a simple field decision, Gomez, and a practical one. Sidelining you for a few hours gave me the headstart I needed."

"And obviously you've done a splendid job." He was upright now, still holding on to the wall.

"As you've also ended up here, I'd say that neither one of us has done especially well."

He glanced around the small room, moving his head carefully so that none of the pieces of broken crockery that seemed to be clogging his skull would rattle. "A modestly furnished hideaway this."

There was no furniture in the blankwalled room.

"This is, so I was told, an isolation cell in the Berggasse Foundation."

"The fact that you're in here is known," he

pointed out. "Sooner or later some of your agent buddies will spring you."

"I haven't, because of the slightly unorthodox way I've been operating—"

"They consider stungunning your lovable colleagues as unorthodox, do they?"

"I've not kept in close contact with anyone," she said. "By the time they learn I'm here, I may be elsewhere."

"Where will that elsewhere be?"

"I don't have the darndest idea," Jenny admitted. "The only soul I've talked to is a rather meanminded nursebot who brought my lunch. If you want to call apple strudel and hot cocoa lunch."

Holding on to the wall, Gomez walked a few paces. "Did you actually get a chance to talk to the Bonecas?"

"Poor souls, yes." She nodded. "They were blown to glory almost immediately after our conversation."

"That explosion wasn't your work, was it?"

"Of course not. We don't go in for murder or assassination."

"Very humane. Stun hapless ops, but never—"

"This is a very rough business we're in."

"Back to the Bonecas. What did you get out of them?"

"The name of the person who acted as go-between for the person who hired them to build that android replica of Jake Cardigan," she answered. "They claimed, by the way, that they had nothing to do with rigging the andy to function as a kamikaze. They seemed decent folks, some of their puppets were very cute and clever. In fact, it seemed to me that—"

"Who hired them?"

"They were contacted while they were performing here in Vienna some weeks ago. The agent's name is Heinrich Weiner and in his daytime cover identity he sells electric cats at the Dings Flohmarkt. I was enroute to his booth, when—"

"How'd you persuade the Bonecas to confide in you?"

"I bribed them. They were very uneasy, sorry about what they'd gotten mixed up in and afraid that someone might eventually try to silence them."

"Did you talk to Weiner at all?"

"No, I was in the process of doing that when I started experiencing some very unpleasant hallucinations. You figured in them, to give you some notion of how unpleasant."

Gomez sighed. "Then we don't know who was behind Weiner."

"The person you want is Professor Nister," said a voice from the ceiling speaker. "You'll be seeing him shortly."

Jake walked briskly along the twilight street. He was dressed in a conservative business suit and carried a medical bag. When he was still a half block from the entrance to the Berggasse Foundation, someone called to him softly from the shadows beside a decorative tree.

"Hey, Cardigan."

He stopped, frowning in the direction of the shadowy figure. "I am much afraid, dear lady, that you've made some mistake," he said in passable German. "I am Dr. Witmann, enroute to visit a patient of mine at the—"

"How'd you like to find out about Gomez?"

Jake moved closer to the large tree. Overhead a skyvan passed, flashing bright lights and playing loud brassy martial music. He waited until it was some distance away, then said, "Is that you, Eva?"

"Quit behaving like a nearsighted wampus, Jake," advised the hefty detective. "You saw me in Greater Los Angeles not more than two months ago, when—"

"Tell me about Gomez."

She jerked her thumb at the 5-story domed building. "They've got him locked up inside there someplace. Didn't you know?"

"I didn't even know he was in Vienna."

"She's in there, too. That skinny secret agent. Jenny Keaton."

Jake swung the medical bag against his leg. "I'm fairly certain a gent named Professor Nister is holed up in there as well."

"That polecat. I've long suspected he's subsidized by one of the more successful Tek cartels."

Jake requested, "Fill me in, briefly, on Sid and Jenny."

"I'm nothing if not terse." She gave him a concise account of what had been going on, concluding with, "I've been hanging around out here casing the setup. Then I was going to contact Bascom or—"

"I'll take care of this."

"Need me to tag along as backup?"

"Nope, wait out here. I'm going in as Dr. Witmann."

"Let's hope you come out again," she said.

═ 39 ═

"MUCH COZIER THAN our former quarters," observed Gomez, scanning the room where they'd just been left by two burly nursebots.

There were a desk, three armchairs and a carpet with an animated leaf pattern. Against one wall was a holographic projection of a deep fireplace and a stack of blazing logs.

"I don't feel especially cozy." Jenny wandered along the edge of the flickering carpet.

One of the walls made a loud, grinding noise and then a panel, rattling, slid aside.

A gaunt, grey man came rolling into the room and the panel, with much noise, shut behind him.

He was attached to a complex electronic wheelchair. Several colored tubes and wires coiled out of the chromed metal framework of the chair and a half dozen plazsax hung from various hooks on it. The majority of tubes and wires were connected to the flesh of the man in the chair. His stick-thin bare arms were festooned with them and there were bruises and red splotches indicating earlier insertions. Dials and gauges, buttons and lights thickly encrusted the frame of the chair.

"Good evening, Fräulein Keaton and Herr Gomez." His voice came out of a small speaker that dangled from the breast pocket of his sleeveless tunic. Held tightly in his skeletal left hand was a silverplated lazgun. "I am Professor Nister. Since you're not local residents, you've probably never seen me on my educational—"

"I'm an accredited agent of the United States government," the angry Jenny told him. "You have absolutely no right to—"

"Actually, my dear, you're a poor disturbed young woman named, according to the ID packet you were carrying at the time of your unfortunate public breakdown, Jolline Kurtzman."

"You know darn well who I really am." She moved closer to him. "And I only had that alleged breakdown because you arranged to have a rigged doll shoot me full of hallucination juice. You can't possibly believe that my government won't move to—"

"Your government, child, will never find so much as a speck of you, Fräulein. You're a loose end that will shortly be completely tidied up."

A small bead of light on the right side of his chair began flashing red. "Excuse me a moment, please." He raised his gun, pointing it directly at her. With the spidery grey fingers of his other hand he reached up to squeeze a plastic sack of greenish liquid that hung on the chair frame. After a few seconds the red light ceased blinking.

"You're not in especially good shape, prof," mentioned Gomez. "A lengthy stay in the hoosegow is going to be very painful for you."

"I shan't be languishing in any prison, Herr Gomez," Nister assured him. "You'll be vanishing as thoroughly as the Fräulein here."

"Possibly, but the Cosmos Agency, unlike most of the slipshod government agencies in my native land, is neither dense nor easily dissuaded," he informed the gaunt man. "With or without my mortal remains to inspire them, they're going to track you down and—"

"Nonsense." Harsh laughter trickled out of the dangling speaker. "Your partner, Herr Cardigan, is a hotheaded fool, whom we've been able to lead a—"

The wall behind him made a loud grinding noise, then the panel, rattling loudly, started to jiggle open.

Surprised, Professor Nister turned to look back at the wall.

Gomez lunged, kicked and booted the lazgun clean out of the thin knobby hand.

Nister yelped in pain. As he brought his injured hand up toward his chest, he managed to detach two tubes and a wire.

Gomez snatched up the fallen gun and aimed it at the widening opening in the wall.

"Relax, Sid," advised Jake as he stepped into the room. "It's me—the hotheaded fool."

It was a nearly smogless night and Greater Los Angeles's multitude of lights glittered sharply below them as they flew toward the Westwood Sector.

Leaning back in her skycab seat, Molly said, "Well?"

Dan was sitting hunched. His right hand was in his jacket pocket clutching the small soundrod he'd borrowed from his father's kit. "Huh?"

"By now you ought to have commented on how terrific I look," she told him.

"You look terrific."

She was wearing a simple black gown made of Moon Base fabric. "More importantly for our cause, I look acceptably Upper Class," the darkhaired young woman added.

"And I don't?"

She waggled her left hand in the air. "Borderline," she told him. "But with me at your side, they'll never suspect that you're not somebody."

"Thanks."

Molly smiled. "Actually, though there's no reason for you to know, I truly am from a very wealthy family," she said. "My father mentioned the last time I saw him, which was the Christmas before last, that he was getting extremely close to his third billion."

"You don't see him much?"

"Not a heck of a lot."

"What about your mother?"

"*My* mother is dead. My father's had, so far as I know, three wives since. It might be four, but I think he would've let me know if there was yet another new stepmother."

"My mother is . . ." He let the sentence die.

"I know."

"She's in jail, awaiting trial."

Nodding, Molly touched his hand.

"I haven't visited her," he said finally.

Molly leaned closer, lowering her voice. "I've been doing some extra research on my own."

"You and Rex, you mean?"

"No, using a private computer setup I sometimes have access to." Molly glanced at the back of their cabbie's head. A sheet of tinted plastiglass separated them from him. "This one belongs to an old friend of my father's who's . . . shady. But then, so is my father."

"You dig up something more about Knerr?"

"About Roddy Pickfair," she said. "I'm not certain what it means, but his birth records are fake."

"How so?"

"He wasn't born where he claimed and the orphanage he's supposed to have been raised in actually only added his name to their back files some five years ago."

"Have you found out anything about who he really is?"

She shook her head. "It was tough enough getting at what I did," she said. "But I should, if I keep using my considerable investigative skills, eventually discover—"

"Be careful."

"I always am."

"If Pickfair is involved in this—then killing people doesn't bother the guy."

"I'm flattered," she said, laughing. "You actually care about me and don't want me to get killed."

"I'd feel responsible," he said.

— ≡ 40 ≡ —

PROFESSOR NISTER, SKELETAL hands shaking, reinserted the tubes and wires into his arms. "I didn't expect you to find me, Herr Cardigan," he said in a perplexed tone. "How did you manage it?"

"Your mistress has been calling you here frequently the past few days." Jake stood facing him. "I persuaded her vidphone to divulge the list of her recent calls."

"That's impossible, every phone has a—"

"Jake is pretty handy at impossible technological feats," explained Gomez, smiling. "We learned a lot of useful tricks back when we were SoCal cops."

"Once I got in here, I worked on your central computer," added Jake, "until it confided in me where exactly you were holed up."

"Now here's a man who gets things done, Gomez," said Jenny, a faint trace of admiration sounding in her voice. "As soon as he found out that we were captives, he took swift action to—"

"Actually I had no idea Nister had grabbed you," he told her. "I was heading here to question him, when I ran into Eva Kraft and she filled me in."

"I have no intention, Herr Cardigan, of answering any—"

"You're the one who arranged to have the android dupe of me constructed and delivered to Berlin, aren't you?"

Jenny said, "He has to be, because he's been trying to keep me from finding out who the Bonecas were really working for."

"To keep *us* from finding out, *chiquita*," corrected Gomez.

Leaning down, Jake inquired, "Did you hire them?"

"You, none of you, seem to realize how powerful the Tek cartel I represent is," the professor told them. "What's happened to you thus far is nothing compared to the vengeance that will be—"

"You're dependent on this chair for your life," observed Jake quietly, leaning even closer to him. "And without any of your toadies or your lazgun—hell, you're at a definite disadvantage, Professor." He straightened up, took a few steps back and studied the chair. "Did you hire the Bonecas?"

Nister made no reply.

Grabbing hold of a tangle of wires and tubes, Jake said, "You don't want all these pulled out—do you?"

The professor ran his tongue over his thin grey lips. "No," he said, his voice coming thin and whispery out of the dangling speaker. "I hired them."

"Whose decision was it to have Beth Kittridge killed?"

"The woman had knowledge of her father's anti-Tek system. According to our information, she was very close to having it ready to go. That would, of course, have meant the destruction of nearly all the Tek chips in the world," Professor Nister said. "It was decided that killing her was absolutely necessary, since it will set anti-Tek research back months at the very least. That was a sound business decision."

"Who gave the order?"

"There was a vote, a unanimous vote by the directors of our cartel."

"I want all their names."

"I can't give—"

"Sure, you can." Jake tightened his grip on the tubes and wires. One of them popped free of the gaunt man's arm and thick yellowish fluid started dribbling out of it and splashing on the floor.

"All right, yes." Seven names came rattling out of the speaker.

"I've got them." Jenny was holding a tiny voxrecorder in her hand.

"Was anyone else involved in the decision to kill Beth?"

Nister's eyes lowered and he watched the yellow liquid slowly dripping. "I can not give—"

"Anyone else?" Jake let go of the tubes and wires to take hold of the front of his tunic. He pulled him halfway up out of his chair. "Was anyone else involved?"

Nister's face turned a paler grey and he started making harsh gagging sounds deep in his throat.

"C'mon! I want an answer!"

Gomez caught Jake's arm. "Easy, *amigo*," he warned. "The guy's speaker got detached." He reconnected it.

"Pickfair," gasped Nister. "Roddy Pickfair. He made the suggestion to us initially. And he masterminded other things."

"What other things?" Jake let go of him.

Professor Nister fell back into the chair, pulling out another tube. He slumped, saying, "The things that happened to you in Brazil."

Jenny asked him, "How did you know when Beth Kittridge and the others would be arriving at the court?"

"We were informed."

"Who?"

"The man's name is Maxwell Junger."

Gomez said, "Head of the IDCA office here in colorful old Vienna."

"Yes, darn it."

Jake was watching Nister's face. "I loved Beth Kittridge," he told him in a jagged voice. "And you voted to kill her. Not just to kill her, but to destroy her body by—"

"Surely, Herr Cardigan, to a man of your long experience in the real world, our methods shouldn't be that shocking."

"You bastard!" Jake thrust his stungun into his belt and took hold of the tubes and wires with both hands. "In the real world I think you ought to die!"

"Jake!" Gomez caught his arm again.

"Please," begged the professor out of the dangling speaker. "I had no choice. If the death vote hadn't been unanimous, then I myself . . ."

Jake took an enormous breath in, held it for a full half minute and then let it go sighing harshly out. His fingers went wide and he dropped all the wires and tubing. "Hell," he said, turning away, "let somebody else kill you."

⎯⎯⎯ **41** ⎯⎯⎯

ALL THE ROBOT waiters, all two dozen of them, were goldplated. They circulated, gracefully, through the crowds at the edges of the vast ebony dance floor. The eighteen-piece orchestra, a mix of human and android musicians, sat on a sparkling silver platform that floated fifteen feet above the hundreds of dancers. At the far end of the Main Ballroom of the GLA Civic Plaza rose a 30-foot-high holographic projection of an injured soldier in the uniform of the UN Brazil Wars forces.

"That was mineral water, sir?" a sleek golden servobot was inquiring of Dan.

"Two." He and Molly were standing very close together on the righthand side of the dance floor, surrounded by dozens of handsome, fashionable elbows and backs.

A compartment in the waiter's gold chest slid open and he withdrew a plazglass from it. Holding it under his right forefinger, he filled it with sparkling mineral water. He handed the glass to Dan, who handed it to Molly, and filled a second one. "There's no tipping allowed," reminded the waiter as he shut his chest and moved on.

"I wasn't planning any."

Molly touched her glass to his. "Cheers. Do you see any of them?"

"Not yet."

"This is going to be difficult—even for someone as astute as me."

"What we'd better do is slowly circle—wait. Look."

"Where?"

"Those tables across the floor, at the one nearest the viewindow."

"Right, that's definitely China Vargas and Roddy Pickfair sitting there."

Dan said, "I think if we move over to the hologram stage, we can hide in the shadows behind it and not be noticed. Then I'll aim the soundrod and—"

"Hey, there's Knerr. He's joining them." She took hold of Dan's arm and started leading him along the edge of the dance floor toward the giant projection of the wounded soldier some hundred yards away. "Excuse us. Sorry. Pardon me."

"Molly Fine! How great." A handsome young

man was standing directly in their path. "I had
no idea you'd—"

"Nice running into you, Len. Right now,
though, I really—"

"Nope, I insist on one dance immediately."

"Maybe later."

"I'll follow you around, dog your every foot-
step, Moll, until—"

"Okay, all right. One." She let go of Dan.
"You go ahead. I'll pacify this nuisance and
join you."

Dan waited until the handsome young man
had taken Molly out into the dancing crowd
and then continued on his way.

In less than five minutes he was crouching
behind the platform, hidden in the deep shadows. He could see the table where China, Knerr
and Pickfair were seated. Carefully he aimed
his soundrod, stuck the tiny earphone in place
and activated the recorder.

". . . something can be arranged," Knerr was
saying.

Pickfair laughed. "Something unpleasant,"
he suggested. "You know, the thing that absolutely annoys the very hell out of me is people
who think that they're smarter than I." He was
a pudgy young man with curly brown hair,
about nineteen at most, and wearing a too tight
tuxsuit.

China took a sip of her drink. "You tend to
get awfully nasty when you're annoyed."

"I'm nasty at the best of times, dear heart."

Smiling, he shifted in his chair and looked directly at the distant spot where Dan was crouched. "You may as well come join us, Danny boy," he said. "We already have Molly."

Gomez, limping slightly, walked over to the window of their hotel suite. A new day was commencing and Vienna was beginning to fill with pale sunlight. "Did you believe the prof?" he asked.

"He impressed me as being sincere, yeah." Jake was sitting, slouched, in an armchair. Weariness showed in his face. "Soon as we finish up the official rigamarole with the local police, I want to head back to Greater LA and look up this Roddy Pickfair."

Turning his back on the morning, Gomez said, "Our assignment, far as Cosmos is concerned, was to find out who was behind the assassinations in Berlin and if any US gov agencies were tied in. We've got Nister, who helped arrange the details of the killings, and eventually we'll have his Tek cartel cronies. We also have the name of the IDCA agent who—"

"It isn't over for me, Sid," said Jake quietly. "Not until I run down everyone who had anything to do with Beth's death."

"Jenny Keaton is planning to remain here in Vienna to see that all the local miscreants get rounded up and brought to justice," reminded his partner. "We can go home to GLA, *sí*, but why don't we just take a rest and—"

"I *didn't* kill Nister last night." Jake rose up out of the chair. "I'm not an uncontrollable madman. If Pickfair is guilty of anything, I won't slaughter him or—"

"You came damn close to doing in Nister, *amigo*." Gomez held his thumb and forefinger an inch apart. "Damn close. I know what you're feeling, but it would be safer to declare this case closed."

"All I intend to do is find out if Pickfair is tied in or not. You don't have to help," Jake told him. "But I'm not stopping. If Bascom wants me to take a leave while I continue to—"

"Jake, *momentito*," cut in his friend. "I'll keep working with you on this mess. But, *por favor*, you have got to stop acting so much like a vigilante. To me you seem to be getting damn close to the edge."

"Maybe I should've reserved a room there at the Berggasse Foundation, huh?" Jake's voice was getting near being a shout. "I've got this problem, doctor. Ever since they blew up Beth, I don't know, I've been upset. Then, after they killed her, they tried to make me believe she was still alive. Why'd they do that? Oh, because it amused the bastards to play a god damn game with—"

"I know what they did. I know what it means to you," said Gomez carefully. "But I don't want to see you turn into somebody who uses a tragedy as an excuse to—"

"Sid, I didn't kill Nister, remember? I wanted to—yeah, I admit that I truly did—but I got control of myself. Even if you hadn't been there, I don't think I would have gone ahead with it."

The vidphone rang.

"I'll answer." Gomez crossed to the alcove. "Then afterwards we can resume hollering at each other, *amigo*."

It was Bascom, even more rumpled than usual. "Is Jake around?"

"Something wrong, *jefe?*"

"Well, something is very much futzed up. Can I—"

"What is it, Walt?" Jake sat down in front of the phonescreen.

"I thought I'd better let you know this," said the head of the Cosmos Detective Agency. "May not be serious, yet—"

"Is it Dan? Has something happened to him?"

"The op who was watching him—it was McCay on this particular shift—was found unconscious, stungunned, in some decorative shrubs behind the GLA Civic Plaza an hour ago."

"And Dan?"

Bascom's shoulders rose and fell. "No trace of him," he answered.

— 42 —

GOMEZ SNAPPED HIS suitcase shut, took a final slow look around the living room of the suite. "Lately, *amigo*, I seem to be continually taking my leave of hotel rooms," he said. "And if I'm not doing that, then I'm acting as a target for stungun practice."

"You were also bitten by a robot dog," reminded Jake. "That was a little out of the ordinary and proves you're not in a complete rut."

The door buzzed.

Walking toward it, Gomez observed, "This is probably some stray hound come to take a nip out of me." He opened the door wide. "Worse."

"Mornings are not your best time," said Jenny Keaton as she came striding into the room.

"I appreciate your dropping by to inform me of that fact."

"Something's come up."

Gomez backed out of her way. "Such as?"

"You're going to have to postpone your departure," the blonde agent informed them. "That's what I came over to—"

"We're leaving for Greater LA in just over an hour," said Jake. "My son is—"

"A special Internal Security investigator is due in Vienna late this afternoon." She stopped beside Gomez's lone suitcase and tapped at it with her boot toe. "My agency insists that you two stand by to make in-person statements to Agent Reisberson."

"That won't be possible," Jake told her.

"That wouldn't be Walter Truett Reisberson, would it?" Gomez gradually eased around until he was standing behind Jenny. "One of my dearest chums in nursery school was named—"

"No, this is Olaf Reisberson."

"It doesn't matter what the hell his name is," said Jake, angry. "Sid and I are—"

"You can't refuse a request such as this," she said to Jake, a frown deepening on her forehead.

Very quietly Gomez drew out his stungun. Pointing it at her back, he fired.

As Jenny started to fall over, he caught her. "Get the bedroom door, *por favor,* Jake."

"I think this is a federal offense." Jake yanked the door open.

"Which? Putting a government agent to bed?"

"Shooting one."

"Really? You think there might be a rule against such behavior?"

"Well, you know how fussy they can get in Washington."

Gomez, gently, placed Jenny flat out on his bed. *"Hasta la vista,"* he muttered. Returning to the living room, he sat down at the vidphone. "Desk, please."

"Ja, Herr Gomez?" said the polite silvery robot who materialized on the screen.

"There's been a slight change of plans," he told the hotel clerk. "I won't be checking out until nine this evening."

"I fear, in that case, we'll be forced to bill you for another full—"

"Perfectly fair. Just charge it to the Cosmos Detective Agency, as usual," said Gomez, smiling cordially. "Ah, and since I'll be taking a nap, don't disturb me."

"As you wish, Herr Gomez."

"But promptly at eight this evening, send up a bellbot to my bedroom to awaken me."

"You wish him to come right in?"

"Exactly, because I'm an extremely heavy sleeper. Have the robot march right in and give a holler."

"Very good, *mein herr.* And what of Herr Cardigan? Will he be staying on and napping or—"

"He'll be checking out as planned." Gomez

ended the call and gathered up his suitcase. "Let's slip unobtrusively out the back way, keeping our eyes out for any stray US government agents who might be hanging around."

"Good idea."

Glancing at the shut bedroom door, Gomez said, "Now we're even, *chiquita.*"

Leaning back in his skyliner seat, Gomez said, "You're not following my example, Jake. You aren't relaxing."

"Damn it, I'm worried about Dan."

"So am I, *amigo.* But all the fretting and fidgeting in the world isn't going to get us to Greater LA ahead of the plane."

Jake had the window seat and was looking absently out at the afternoon sky. "It's just that it seems like they're out to get everyone who's close to me," he said, twisting his hands together. "Now, if they kill Dan—"

"They won't do that. Not yet anyway."

"There's no way you can be sure of that."

"They have two ways of working, these *cabróns.* Either they strike at once without warning, or they tease and torture for awhile," observed his partner. "I'm betting Dan's alive."

Jake said, "Roddy Pickfair fits into this someplace, too."

"It's my impression that young Roddy is a silent partner in their Tek cartel—make that *was,* since that Vienna-based bunch is pretty much defunct."

"Soon as we—"

"Pardon me, Mr. Cardigan." A robot attendant had halted in the aisle.

"Yeah?"

"There's a satphone call for you," explained the robot. "If you'll come to the lounge?"

"Is it about my son?"

"I have no idea."

Jake worked his way into the aisle and walked back to the lounge. Stepping into the phone alcove, he sat.

"Hi, pal. Remember me?"

Jake studied the copperplated robot on the screen. "You're Rex/GK-30. What—"

"Listen, kiddo, I'm not supposed to make calls like this," explained Rex, glancing around. "It could put my toke in a sling, so I got to talk fast before any of the school brass get wise."

"You're at the academy now—is this about Dan?"

"You got it, boss."

"Do you know where he is?"

"Not exactly, but I'm working on it. Meantime, I wanted to pass along what I do know. I was going to spill this to Bascom over at Cosmos, but then I got wind you and Gomez were heading home via skyliner."

"Okay, what do you have?"

"Your offspring, along with a bright kid named Molly Fine, have been digging into the life and times of several parties," explained

Rex. "I have been, unbeknownst to the mucks around here, lending a hand."

"Which parties?"

"They commenced with Larry Knerr, then branched out to Roddy Pickfair—and China Vargas," the robot informed him. "Plus which, Molly's been using sources of her own to delve further into the background of Pickfair. She's come up with the fact that his birth records are phony, but I don't know where that leads anybody."

"Do you know why they were at the GLA Civic Plaza?"

"Yeah, sure. That was my fault in a way," answered Rex/GK-30. "There was a big charity shindig there and Dan found out that Pickfair, Knerr and the Vargas frail were all going to attend. They talked me into getting them, by using a few electronic dodges, onto the guest list. Dan was planning to eavesdrop on the group, using some surveillance gadgets borrowed from your collection and—"

Rex was all at once gone from the screen. Now the face of an angry, thickset man of fifty appeared. "The conversation is over, Cardigan," he announced.

"Put Rex back on, Farber," requested Jake evenly.

"Rex is on suspension as of now," Dick Farber told him. "It's damned lucky I came along and discovered this before too much classified information got out."

"You must know that my son's missing," said Jake. "Rex has information that might—"

"If your kid is really missing, Cardigan, and not just shacked up with the Fine girl, the proper authorities will be supplied with whatever the academy deems useful to them," said Farber. "Notice that I said *proper* authorities. That sure as hell doesn't include excons working as cheap gumshoes. So long, jerk."

The screen went blank.

—≡ 43 ≡—

THERE WAS DAN on the wall.

Caught for a moment by a roving robot news-cam that had attended the charity ball at the GLA Civic Plaza on behalf of Newz, Inc.

Bascom touched a button, freezing the image on the large vidscreen. "The pretty lass tugging at his arm is Molly Fine," he said. "We did some digging into her background after you passed on Rex/GK-30's tip, Jake. Very intelligent, very rich. Only daughter of Gilbert Fine, the servomech billionaire."

"Is he linked with Tek in any way?" Jake was sitting on the edge of one of the agency chief's office chairs.

"Not that we can find. Pop Fine is pretty much a scoundrel, but in the traditional big business mode."

Gomez was hunkered deep down in a soft chair, knees up and chin low. "Who's the lad who's blocking their progress?"

"We've tentatively identified him as Len O'Hearn, of the O'Hearn satcom family. Also very rich, though not especially intelligent."

Jake said, "So now we know for sure that Dan and Molly were there."

"And there's ample footage of Pickfair, Knerr and the hairless China," added Gomez.

"We also know," said Bascom, starting up the film again, "that Molly danced with the O'Hearn heir. You'll note that she's moving into the fray with him."

"I also note Dan giving O'Hearn a very uncordial glare before being swallowed up by the crowd."

"The fabled Cardigan glare." Gomez sank further into his chair.

"We did an earlier scan of all this material," said Bascom, stopping it. "What you fellows have just watched is all there is of Dan and Molly—and of the Pickfair trio."

"What time was that last?"

"The stuff on Dan and Molly was shot at 9:47 that evening."

"And what time was McCay stungunned?"

"Approximately ten P.M."

"So we can't trace Dan or the girl after that?"

"Not as yet," said the agency head. "We also have another problem."

Jake stood. "Which is?"

"We haven't been able to locate Roddy Pickfair, Larry Knerr or China Vargas."

"What does the Ampersand studio say?"

"That Mr. Pickfair is out of town, but they don't know where," answered Bascom. "Obviously I've got people working on locating the lad."

"What's the *GLA Fax-Times* have to say?"

"The senior Vargas is vacationing in Mexico. His daughter is not at the newspaper offices nor at the family home in the Bel Air Sector," continued Bascom. "Knerr is supposedly off covering a story, but they have no information on his current whereabouts."

"Dan and Molly must be with one of them," said Jake, starting to pace the big office. "We've got to find them."

"What about the minions of the law?" inquired Gomez. "What are they up to?"

"The Greater Los Angeles cops aren't taking this very seriously as yet," said Bascom. "It's their opinion that Dan and Molly probably just decided to sneak away somewhere after the dance and haven't gotten around to letting anyone know."

"Dan isn't like that," said Jake, angry. "And how the hell do they explain McCay's getting gunned down?"

"They suggest that's a simple mugging—his valuables *were* swiped—not necessarily connected with the other business," said Bascom.

"Keep in mind, Jake, that from a jaded policeman's point of view, it's more likely that the kids just took off to fool around someplace. And as far as the SoCal State Police are concerned, they can't rule this a kidnapping for two more days. Them's the rules."

"Video." Gomez was gazing at the blank wallscreen.

Jake scowled at him. "What?"

Gomez shifted in his chair, rolled his eyes, made a strange clucking noise with his tongue. "I was just now visited with an odd notion as I sat slumped here." He came slowly up out of the depths of the chair. "As I watched the dark-haired Molly, I was suddenly wafted back to that fateful day when we were all gathered 'round watching the dying message from Jean Marie Sparey."

"And?"

Gomez shook his head in a perplexed way. "Something flickered across the barren landscape of my mind," he answered finally. "I had the sudden feeling that I'd seen the young lady somewhere before. Though at the time I didn't realize it, not consciously anyway."

"She's Will Sparey's daughter, you probably saw her when she was a kid."

"You and Sparey were pals, I wasn't a chum of his," reminded Gomez. "Besides which, that *muchacha* probably wasn't the true Jean Marie anyway."

Jake said, "You're probably right, yeah. But what—"

"She was no doubt a ringer, an imposter, an . . . *Caramba!* She was an actress." He walked over to Bascom, held out his hand. "Can you provide me with a copy of that sentimental vidcaz, *jefe?*"

"Surely, but what in the—"

"I'm suddenly curious to find out what's become of her since she was pulled back from the jaws of death down in Rio," he told them. "Jake, I'd like to fool around with this for awhile. Okay?"

"Fine, I have a few things I want to work on," he said. "We'll keep in touch through the office here."

Bascom said, "I'd feel considerably better if I knew what the hell either of you was talking about."

"You remember him fondly, am I right?"

Gomez shook his head. "I remember him not at all, Wolfe."

Wolfe Bosco's face puckered. "You're spoofing me, is that it?"

"Suppose we move on to business?"

The small redhaired agent pointed again toward the tiny kitchen of his apartment on the topmost floor of the four-story Palm Oasis Apartments in the heart of the Hollywood Sector of GLA. "Why, that's Jacko Fuller."

An android simulacrum was busily fixing

sandwiches in the kitchen. "Maybe if I sing it'll refresh his memory, Wolfe."

"Just keep working on the sandwiches, schmuck," advised the agent. "Jacko Fuller, Gomez? This one is the best surviving public appearance andies. The rest tend to sing off key."

"I don't recall his career. Now can ⸺"

"Three years as featured vocalist on *Mud-wrestling Melodies*. Surely you watched that as an unfortunate child growing up in ethnic squalor in some trashy⸺"

"Wolfe, I came here prepared to pay you a handsome fee for information." He took a vid-caz from his jacket pocket.

"The real Jacko Fuller is now a gibbering geek in a senior enclave in the San Diego Sector. I find that sad, very sad."

"It's not that cheering that you have his sim doing your housework."

"We take turns. Him and me and Deb. You, am I right, fondly recall Deb Brophy, the Sax Queen of the Ice Rink and⸺"

"No."

"What a bleak childhood you must've had. It no doubt has blighted your adult life, am I right about that?"

"Shall I make extra sandwiches for our guest, Wolfe?"

"No, nope." Gomez dropped the cassette back in his pocket.

"I can activate Deb, would you like that,

Gomez?" asked the agent. "When you hear her belt out a blues on the alto, you'll probably remember enjoying—"

"We hocked her horn," reminded the android from the kitchen.

"She can still hum. What a talented performer Deb was," said Bosco. "The real Deb fried her brains with Tek and conked off about six years back in Mentor, Ohio. But she lives on right here in my talent stable, ready to bring joy to—"

"I'm trying to find someone." Gomez caught him by both arms. "With your vast knowledge of show business, Wolfe, I hoped you'd be able to help me out. However, all you've done thus far is try to interest me in superannuated andies and—"

"What sort of fee is involved in this transaction? The Cosmos outfit provides you, I'm fully aware, with an eyepopping expense account."

"I'm offering $100."

"Outlandish. An insult. Did you hear that, Jacko?"

"An insult for sure, Wolfe. A slap in the face."

"Gomez, I'd have to have, at the very least— $500."

"$200 and no more."

"Did you happen to overhear this latest offensive suggestion, Jacko?"

"I did. I'm astonished."

"*Adiós,* Wolfe. You, too, Jacko."

"I'll lower my fee to $250."

"$200."

"That's virtually nothing. I'll take it, however."

Gomez produced the cassette again and handed it to the agent. "I think the lady seen hereon is a smalltime actress who may possibly reside in GLA somewhere," he told Wolfe Bosco. "I have the vague impression I may even have seen her in some small role about a year or so ago. Unfortunately that notion only recently dawned on me."

After rubbing the cassette on the elbow of his plaid jacket, the agent walked over to the player that sat on his lamé coffee table. "If the frail has ever trod the boards, I'll know her."

"He's known far and wide," called Jacko from the kitchen, "as the Walking Encyclopedia of Show Biz Lore."

"That's true," admitted Bosco, "entirely true." He inserted the vidcaz.

Nothing happened.

"Function." He whapped the machine with his fist.

Up on the dirt-smeared wallscreen appeared Jean Marie Sparey. "They're letting me make this . . . I sure hope . . . you can come see me . . . Uncle Jake . . . I'm a real mess, huh? It's . . . it's mostly from doing Tek . . . had a lot of seizures and . . . I really . . . truly . . . futzed up my body and . . . anyway, please . . . I must . . . talk to you."

Bosco turned off the machine, made a loud snuffling noise, wiped at the corner of his eye. "Touching. What a perf."

"Moving," called Jacko, "judging from the audio."

"Do you know who she is, Wolfe?" asked Gomez.

"Sure, that was Susan Ferrier. I didn't know the kid had that much talent. Tears to my eyes is what she brought. I should be representing her."

"A terrific idea," said Jacko. "She'd be perfect for the lead in—"

"Where can I find her?"

"You want an identification *and* a current address—all for a pitiful $200, am I right about that?"

"That's absolutely right, *sí.*"

"Very well." He worked his way over to his phone. "I'll find out for you, Gomez, where the quiff is right this very moment. But there's no denying that I've fallen from greatness."

"It's a tragedy, a modern day tragedy," said Jacko, finishing up the sandwiches.

—=44=—

AUNT ELSIE LIT her cigar, took a slow puff and then chuckled out smoke. "You're looking just great, Jake."

"Am I?"

"Well, as a matter of fact, no. You look like they left you out all night in the rain. You didn't come here as a customer, did you?"

He was sitting in a frilly armchair in Aunt Elsie's office. The office was furnished much like a parlor of at least a century earlier. "Nope, I came to question one of your clients."

Aunt Elsie was a thin woman in her late forties. Her pale blonde hair was cut short and she wore a grey business suit. "Jake darling, the Past Recaptured Bordello is the most exclusive—*and* expensive—whorehouse in Greater

Los Angeles," she told him, sighing out smoke. "I wouldn't think of disturbing a customer, not even for a cherished old friend like you."

He left his chair to approach her handcarved desk. "My son is missing, probably kidnapped," he told her. "I think a young man named Len O'Hearn may know something about—"

"But *he's* not the one who's here, darling. It's his father, Rian O'Hearn, the—"

"Len has dropped from view. I'm betting his father can tell me where to find him."

She took a careful drag on the thin cigar. "This is Danny you're talking about?"

"Dan, yeah."

"How old is he?"

"Fifteen."

"Is he? Seems like just the other day you were telling me that your wife was expecting. That was when I had my place in the Laguna Sector and you and Gomez dropped in to shut me down for awhile," she said. "Fifteen years ago or more that must've been."

"I can wait outside until he comes out, but it would be helpful if I could see him sooner."

"How'd you find out Rian was at my establishment?"

Jake smiled. "Sources."

"He's an interesting customer," said Aunt Elsie, leaning back in her desk chair. "What we've re-created for him is the lady who taught him English Lit in junior college thirty some years ago. Rather a plain woman, if you want my opinion, but he seems to enjoy coming here once each week to sleep with our android sim. It also pleases him to do that in a replica of the bedroom he had when he was a kid in the Hawthorne Sector of—"

"Something terrible." A lean black man stepped into the office through the wall panel that had just snapped open.

"What is it, Edmond?"

"It's Rian O'Hearn," he answered nervously. "The man's suffered some sort of attack. I sent our medibot up to attend him, but I think you best have a look, ma'am."

"I'll look, too," Jake said.

Gomez came strolling in out of the late afternoon sunshine. He smiled amiably at the slim, darkhaired young woman behind the wide ivory reception desk.

"You got here just in time, sir," she informed him, studying his face. "We can probably still help you. Name, please?"

"Gomez." Settling into the ivory chair facing her desk, he asked, "Are you Amber Alvarez?"

"That's my professional name, yes."

"You're the very person I'm seeking."

"I am? Are you a producer, director, talent scout or—"

"Not exactly, *chiquita.*" He leaned both elbows on her desk.

"Are you certain you didn't come into NuFaz, Inc., for a new face?"

"I don't need a new one."

"You can't be content with all those wrinkles, pouches and—"

"They give me a seasoned look. How old do you think I am, anyway?"

"Well, it seems to me it would take you at least forty years to do that much damage."

Gomez, frowning, lifted his elbows from her desk. "I'm a few years shy of forty," he said. "Now let's return to the true reason for my visit."

"We can usually help people in advanced stages of trouble such as you, Mr. Sanchez."

"Gomez. I'm not in trouble."

She swung the small vidscreen mounted on her desk around so it was facing him. "I can, at no charge, show you exactly how NuFaz, Inc., can redo your entire face so that you'll look years and years younger and feel more confident about—"

"If I felt any more confident they'd have to strap me down."

"At your age—"

"You're thirty yourself, that's not all that far from—"

"I'm twenty-six."

"C'mon, I've already looked you up."

"Why would you have done that? Just to come in to consult about a makeover doesn't—"

"I don't *want* a makeover," he insisted. "I'm perfectly satisfied with my visage."

"Here. I'll draw your old face on the screen and then demonstrate how we can improve it."

"I'm looking for Susan Ferrier," he said as calmly as possible. "Her talent agency says they've lost touch, but that you, as her current roommate, would know her whereabouts."

"Then you are in the movie industry?"

Gomez eyed the ceiling and made himself look sheepish. "Okay, I guess I'm not too good at concealing it," he said ruefully. "It's important that we locate Susan immediately."

"A part?"

"I can only say that it's the opportunity of a lifetime."

"I look a good deal like her. Except not quite as dark."

He cocked his head, studied her. "You know, Amber— By the way, you wouldn't object, would you, to changing your name?"

"Not at all. To what?"

"Something besides Amber. Anyway, you might be perfect, near perfect at least, for another role in this project. Yes, I can see you as Sister Jonquil."

"This is a religious film, is it?"

"It's inspirational, but not without sufficient sex and violence," he explained. "The thing is, Amber, we can't go ahead until we sign Susan. She's pivotal to the entire costly venture."

"Boy, she's sure been having a lot of luck lately. First that part in Brazil and then that other job."

"What other job?"

"The one she's working on right now."

"Where?"

"On location."

"Pin it down a bit more."

"She's in NorCal. She got a great part on *Jungle Commandos*. That's a new big budget Brazil War film that Ampersand is doing."

"Ampersand, of course." He nodded sagely. "Where exactly in NorCal?"

"I think she's at the Dickerson Jungle Park in Sonoma, Mr. Gomez," answered Amber. "That's where they're shooting the jungle warfare stuff. She was supposed to go up there two days ago, but I haven't heard from her since."

"The jungle will serve as a good starting point." He stood. "In case she contacts you, don't mention my interest."

"But if you're anxious to—"

"I don't want anyone talking about the project until I can nail down her participation."

"Can you send me a script?"

He patted his chin. "Do you really think my face needs improving?"

"No, not really, Mr. Gomez. I was only kidding with you earlier."

"I'll be in touch." He hurried from the office.

Rian O'Hearn, eyes closed and breathing in short choppy gasps, was sprawled faceup on the replica of his boyhood bed.

A naked female android sat, hands folded in

her lap, in a chair near the foot of the bed. "It wasn't my fault, Aunt Elsie," she was saying. "It happened, really, before anything happened."

Jake was standing close to the white-enameled medibot who was administering an injection to the ailing man, using the needlegun built into his forefinger.

"How serious?" asked Jake.

"A mild heart attack, brought on by nostalgia mixed with sexual excitement," replied the robot.

"O'Hearn." Jake leaned close.

"It's wiser, sir, not to try to talk to him until the ambulance arrives."

"I only have a few questions."

"It's okay, doc," said Aunt Elsie as she draped a flowered robe over the android's shoulders.

"O'Hearn," repeated Jake.

"Yeah?" he murmured.

"Your son—Len. Where is he?"

"He's a dolt."

"I don't doubt it, but where is he?"

"Running off, when he was supposed to go on a job interview. Dolt."

"Where did he run off to?"

"NorCal. With that gang of movie idiots."

"Where in NorCal?"

"Sonoma. Some jungle park or other." O'Hearn began shivering, coughing.

The medibot urged Jake aside. "That's all for now, sir."

"It's sufficient," said Jake.

— ≡ 45 ≡ —

GOMEZ WAS WHISTLING, sitting comfortably in the passenger seat of the borrowed skyvan. "There's a real difference between NorCal air and SoCal air," he observed as their craft flew through the sunlit morning.

Jake was piloting the craft. "Who used to own this van?"

"I told you, some musical friends of mine," answered his partner. "It's the perfect cover for us to use in penetrating into Northern reaches."

"It smells very odd."

"The group is somewhat old-fashioned. They smoke antique products like marihuana—and they sometimes indulge in bouts of gourmet cooking."

"And the van is gaudy."

"Exactly, *sí,*" agreed Gomez. "Pickfair will expect us to come slinking in, all grey and inconspicuous. We, however, arrive in a purple and crimson skyvan."

Jake said nothing.

Gomez stretched, patting the large crate that rested on the floor behind his seat. "I truly think, *amigo,* that you don't fully appreciate my abilities as a scrounger," he said. "I acquired this impressive van for us, plus the valuable contents of this crate—and that latter chore took much deft dickering."

"You're the ideal partner," said Jake. "Beyond a doubt."

"What's needed on this case is someone capable of outthinking Roddy Pickfair."

"Seems pretty likely that he's got Dan and Molly up there with him in Sonoma," said Jake. "According to the plans of Dickerson's Jungle that we were able to sneak a look at—"

"Again because of one of *my* connections."

"Yep. According to those, there's an entire complex built underground beneath the jungle," continued Jake. "Dan is probably being kept there."

"Mousetrap," said Gomez. "With the kids as bait."

"That's what Pickfair must be feeling at this point."

"We've got to convince the *cabrón,*" said Gomez, "that we're mice."

* * *

The walls were quiet again.

But there was, as always, no way of telling for how long.

Dan and Molly sat side by side on the floor of the enormous room. He had an arm around her shoulders.

The darkhaired young woman had fallen into an uneasy sleep, head resting against his chest, a moment earlier.

Dan's eyes were starting to drift shut. He hadn't slept for more than a few minutes at a time since they'd been put here. However the hell long that was.

Molly was breathing uneasily, making small moaning sounds.

He could feel her heart beating and it seemed to him that it was beating much too rapidly.

Then the pictures came back.

First on the lefthand wall, next on the right. Then the wall in front of them, then on the one in back.

The pictures weren't the worst part, because you could just shut your eyes. But when the sound kicked in there was no escaping.

Sometimes it was so intense that clamping your hands over your ears, even after you'd packed them with wads of torn plyochief, didn't help at all.

The noise level, though, varied. At times the sound was so loud it shook the walls. At others it sank to barely audible.

What the room kept showing them, over and over, was pictures of Beth Kittridge. Pictures of the final minutes of her life.

Closeups, long shots, regular speed, slow motion.

On the righthand wall now Beth was moving toward the android replica of Jake—extremely slowly, seeming to float in his direction. On the lefthand wall loomed a giant image of just her face.

Dan tightened his grip on the fitfully slumbering Molly and closed his eyes.

On the walls Beth was probably moving nearer to the kamikaze android. The one who looked just like Dan's father.

Dan had seen the pictures hundreds of times so far since they'd been brought here. He wasn't certain exactly how long he and Molly had been in this room surrounded by the pictures.

They'd been fed four times and he'd used the screened toilet in the corner five times.

But that wasn't as good a way as a clock to tell time.

Suddenly there was an enormous explosion. It rattled the walls, shook the floor.

Dan knew that if he looked he'd see Beth's body being torn to pieces. On one wall she'd be turning into bloody fragments that ever so slowly scattered across that Berlin morning. On another rushing apart with accelerated swiftness.

Maybe on one wall they would freeze at the moment she started to be ripped apart. Perhaps on another the sequence would reverse and the bloody tatters of flesh and bone and guts would miraculously reunite and form a living, smiling Beth.

Sometimes that last happy moment of her life would repeat and repeat and that final smile would appear and reappear.

Another explosion came, and another.

Molly cried out, jerked awake. "How long have I been asleep?" she asked, lifting her head from his chest.

"Few minutes."

Gently he let go of her. He stood up, staring up at the distant ceiling. "What the hell do you want, you bastards?"

The pictures ceased and the walls were quiet again.

— 46 —

THE PALE GREEN robot was wearing a coarse grey monk's robe and carrying a portable mike. "Unlike real grapes," he was saying to the string of fifteen tourists that was trailing him through the vast domed central building of the Pieters Brothers Winery, "synthetic grapes are not susceptible to weather, air defects, soil deficiencies or any of a multitude of other annoyances. In the vat on your immediate left we're in the process of creating a new batch of our famous aged zinfandel. This complex process takes a full two weeks. In the next vat, ladies and gentlemen . . ."

Jake and Gomez peeled off from the line of tourists and, keeping the huge grey vats between them and the robot guide, headed for an exit.

William Shatner

"If my informant is correct," said Jake once they were out in the late morning, "Larry Knerr is residing in the second of those five rustic cottages yonder."

Across a wide field of imitation grass stood five thatch-roofed cottages in a circle of tall imitation redwoods.

Making their way downhill, the partners circled the cottage they wanted and approached it from the back side.

Gomez scanned the back door, shifting the briefcase he was carrying from his right hand to his left. "Relatively simple alarm system," he observed. "I can disable it in—"

"No, let's use the front way," suggested Jake. "I'm sure Larry will be pleased to see us."

"Where in the blinking hell did you come from?" said the silverhaired reporter when he opened his cottage door and noted them on his doorstep.

Jake pushed him back into the parlor and into a chair. "I'm looking for my son."

"Would I be flaming likely to know where he is? I'm working on a series on the wine country for—"

"Where is he?"

Gomez had entered and shut the door. "Okay, you didn't let me use the electronics stuff," he said. "But, *por favor,* allow me to try the truth kit, Jake."

"We won't need it, Sid. Larry's going to tell us exactly what—"

"I'm going to tell you to take a flapping leap for yourself, Cardigan. I don't know how you located—"

"If what you're worried about, Jake, is that last guy I questioned— Trust me, I figured out since where I went wrong."

"Sooner or later the Austrian police are going to find his body," said Jake, shaking his head. "I don't want to have to explain another foul-up by you."

"It was just that I had the power turned up too high on the prod."

"I thought you told me that what went wrong was too strong a dose of truth serum."

Gomez frowned thoughtfully. "Did I? Well, maybe—"

"People don't usually turn that pasty white color from—"

"What," inquired the uneasy reporter, "did you chaps want to know?"

"Where's Dan?"

Knerr was watching Gomez's briefcase as it swung slowly back and forth. "They've got him and the girl in an underground facility at Dickerson's Jungle," he told them. "Ampersand is shooting *Jungle Commandos* at—"

"We'd like to get into that facility."

"I suppose you would, but you need a special electrokey."

"Loan us yours," requested Gomez, resting his briefcase on the floor.

"I don't have one of the blinking things. They don't trust me that far."

"How about China Vargas?"

"Right you are, she has one."

Jake asked, "Where is she at the moment?"

Gomez smiled. *"Bueno,* I get to use my truth kit after all."

"She's staying at the Vineyard Spa. That's about fifteen miles south of here."

"We'll call on her," said Jake. "But don't you alert her to that fact."

"You have my blinking word, gents."

Nodding, Gomez fished his stungun out of the briefcase and used it.

Large yellow butterflies flickered among the holographic arbors that fronted the Vineyard Spa. The musky scent of ripe golden grapes, pumped discreetly out of tiny nozzles concealed in the artificial loam, was thick in the early afternoon air.

Jake and Gomez had parked the Central Sonoma Sheriff's Office landcar they were now using in a vine-sheltered parking lot below and were riding one of the escalators that climbed up through the simulated grape arbors to the spa. Both wore deputy uniforms.

"Too wide across the shoulders," complained Gomez, moving his left elbow back and forth, "and too long in the leg."

"Act like a deputy sheriff," advised Jake,

"and nobody'll notice that your borrowed uniform doesn't quite fit."

The spa itself consisted of three sprawling buildings made of real adobe and roofed with authentic red tiles.

A broadchested robot in a white smock was sitting in the sunshine near the main entrance. "You boys are new," he commented, looking them over.

"Just got transferred from Marin County," Gomez told him.

"Then you must know a buddy of mine. Alex/CR-70?"

"Can't place him. We're here to see Dr. Howzinger."

"Sure, go on through this door, along the central corridor and it's the second door on your right."

"Much obliged," said Jake.

"Got to stay on the good side of the law," said the robot.

There was a similar robot at the desk in Howzinger's outer office. "Yes?"

Smiling, Gomez yanked out his stungun, fired it and disabled the mechanism.

The robot fell forward on his desk with a loud thunk.

Jake walked over to the inner door and tapped politely.

"What? Now what?"

"Dr. Howzinger, sir?"

"Yes? What? What do you want?"

"Sheriff's Office, sir."

"Sheriff's Office. It's about this crime out here, sir."

"Crime? What the devil are you talking about?" The door was jerked open by a small man with frizzy blond hair. He was about fifty, wearing a suit of a flowery pattern. "Who are you? What are you doing here?"

Jake pointed his thumb at the fallen robot. "Well, Dr. Howzinger, sir," he said, "we got a report about this—I guess you'd classify it manslaughter, although—"

"Manslaughter? Why, that's only Arnie/ID-PR. He's forever toppling over on his—"

"Somebody phoned this in as an assault case, sir," said Gomez. "That's why we rushed over."

"No one phoned this in to anybody. I'm going to get in touch with Sheriff Wollters and—"

"Better not," advised Jake.

"What's that? Are you telling me what I can and can not do?"

"I'm telling you that Sheriff Wollters is likely to say he's never heard of either one of us," Jake explained. "That we probably donned these uniforms as a way of getting in here without any fuss."

"What's that? Who are you? What are you?"

"We're curious." Gomez produced his stungun again.

"And we want to chat with China Vargas."

"Who's that? I've never heard of her."

"Dr. Howzinger, you can tell us what part of

your fashionable establishment she's in—or we can deck you and have your computer tell us."

"Are you threatening me? Is that what you're attempting?"

Gomez sighed and used his stungun. "Go talk to his computer, Jake."

— ⁇ **47** ⁇ —

CHINA VARGAS STUDIED her bald head in the oval enlarging mirror the handsome blond android was holding up to her. "Shit, it looks awful," she remarked.

Making a series of annoyed sounds, she uncoiled up out of the black chair she was sitting in. She walked over to the nearest of the small floating vidscreens, narrowed her eyes to near slots and scrutinized the image.

"Have you got bunting for brains, Hugo?"

"Actually, China, it's a chip augmented with—"

"Look at the simulation of my damn head." Her fingernails made pinging noises as she tapped the screen angrily.

The smocked andy came to her side, rested a

hand on her shoulder. "You aren't getting much out of your relaxation therapy group, dear," he said. "Your snide—"

"Screw the group," she said. "And how can any rational human being relax when they end up with the wrong damn snake tattooed on their own personal skull?"

"Is this a rhetorical question, hon?"

"Can you see the design on the screen, Hugo?" This time she tapped the vidscreen with her clenched fist. "It's a sleek, sensual snake. Whereas the snake that's been etched on my *cabeza* is dumpy and dippy looking."

"They're identical, hon," assured the android. "But, since you're seeing it in reverse in—"

"I should never have had the damn raven removed."

Hugo gave a small polite cough. "Didn't I mention that very thing?"

"Myself, I think it's a great snake." Gomez, gun in hand, had come easing into the small white room and was walking over to them.

Jake followed, shutting the door. "I used to know a guy who had a single rose tattooed on his head. It was subtle."

"Compared to a snake, sure," said Gomez. "Well, China, to business."

Jake approached her. "I'm looking for my son."

"So go look."

His voice was low and level. "I've run out of patience."

"That happened late yesterday," said Gomez. "Sit someplace, Hugo."

"Are we in the midst of some kind of criminal investigation, Sheriff?"

"Sit."

Jake took hold of the bald young woman's arm. "Is Dan being held at the jungle?"

"Yes, both of them are there. Now let go of me."

"Where? In the underground facility?"

"Yes, in Section 4," she answered. "Really now, Cardigan, I'm out of this mess. It's purely a coincidence that I happen to be in the same vicinity."

"What's Pickfair intend to do?"

"Kill them—eventually. He's a very nasty young man."

"We want to get into the underground complex."

"Well, don't let me stand in the way."

"You have an electrokey." He tightened his grip on her arm. "Give it to me."

"I'm sorry I ever hired you two buffoons. You've futzed up my life ever since."

"The key," repeated Jake.

"It's in my jacket pocket. On the hook there."

Gomez frisked the hanging coat. *"Aquí,"* he said, smiling and holding it up.

* * *

The walls had been blank for quite awhile.

"I have a feeling," said Molly, "that something else is getting ready to happen."

Dan said, "I might as well tell you something."

"Don't sound so glum."

"It's just that—well, you haven't really been that much of a nuisance," he told her. "As a matter of fact, I sort of like you."

"Sort of like me?" She laughed. "Here we are on the brink of oblivion and that's the best you can come up with?"

"How can you laugh? We really are going to—probably going to die."

"Well, I sort of like you, too," Molly said. "I prefer to believe that we're at the start of a great romance. Great romances have a tendency to last and endure."

"Not this one, dear," said one of the walls.

That same wall, smoothly and silently, slid aside.

Roddy Pickfair, clad in a loosefitting white suit and with a silver lazgun held loosely in his right hand, was standing widelegged in the corridor outside. "I do hope you enjoyed the picture show, kids," he said. "You knew Beth Kittridge, didn't you, Danny?" he asked. "But, of course, you did. She was scheduled to be your second mom."

Molly took hold of Dan's hand. "Don't," she whispered.

"You've had, I'd venture to say, awfully bad

luck in the mother area. Original one in jail, candidate for #2 shattered to—"

"You son of a bitch," said Dan quietly.

"You're wondering perhaps what's going to happen next?" Pickfair, smiling, came into the room. "That's important in good storytelling— make them ask what's coming next." He walked closer, keeping his gun trained on the young woman. "Allow me to give you some background, fill you in on some of the reasons for what's been going on. For instance, as to the death of Beth Kittridge— By the way, would you like to see that footage again? I had some of my own cambots there, pretending to be with Newz, Inc."

"Dan, stay put." Molly held on to his hand. "Don't let him goad you into anything."

"I know why she was killed," said Dan, strain showing in his voice. "She was close to perfecting an effective anti-Tek system. You must be connected with one of the Tek cartels and—"

"That was one reason, yes." He held up a finger. "Not my only one, however. Beth Kittridge was killed at that particular time and place and in that particular way because I knew it would hurt Jake Cardigan."

"Why do you want to hurt him?"

"Miss Fine can probably guess," he answered. "She's been doing some very annoying rummaging into my background."

Molly said, "It must have something to do with your parents."

"With my *father* actually."

Dan was watching him. "Bennett Sands was your father," he said. "I can see traces of that—hidden in that fat face."

"Officially Sands never had a son," said Molly.

"He and my mother weren't exactly married, but he was my father nonetheless," said Pickfair. "He didn't treat me, admittedly, all that well at first. In later years we became friends, however, and he admired my business sense. I loved him—and Jake Cardigan killed him."

"My father didn't kill him. Someone else entirely was responsible for—"

"If Cardigan hadn't gotten out of the Freezer and started investigating the—"

"Sands was tied in with the Teklords," Dan told him. "Sooner or later he was bound to get killed."

"But he was killed *sooner*—because of your father. What I've been after is revenge."

Molly asked, "What's the next phase of your plan?"

Pickfair strolled over to the lefthand wall. He gestured and it became again a vidscreen.

This time, though, Jake was up there on the screen. Alone, carrying a stungun, he was making his way slowly and cautiously along a metal corridor.

"Cardigan has been led to believe that he's outfoxed me," explained the studio head. "Actually, I've allowed him to get possession of an electrokey for this place. Just four minutes ago he entered this facility. In another two and a half I'll meet him in that corridor—and kill him."

═ **48** ═

SUSAN FERRIER SLIPPED into the large landvan
that served as her dressing room. It was parked,
along with six others, at the edge of a clearing
in the section of the Dickerson Jungle that was
being used as a location for *Jungle Commandos*.

She sank down onto her couch, tugged off her
boots. "Trina?" she called.

Her robot maid didn't respond.

"Damn, is that halfwit on the blink again?"

"She's pretty much defunct." Gomez, smiling
broadly, stepped out of the bathroom.

Susan inhaled sharply and reached toward a
pillow.

"Gun's not there anymore, *chiquita*," the detective informed her.

"You—you're Gomez, aren't you?"

"*Sí*, none other." He sat in a canvas chair, facing her. "I must say you look much better than you did the last time I saw you."

"What do you mean? We've never met."

"But we have, *cara*. Through the magic of video, I was able to see you on your deathbed."

"I'm afraid I don't know what you're talking about."

"*Por favor*, spare me the malarkey." He continued to smile at her. "You undertook the part of Jean Marie Sparey. You played to a very limited audience, but it was undoubtedly lucrative all the same."

"Listen, Gomez, I didn't know they were planning to kill anybody."

"Sure, and they coerced you to take a part in this epic, too."

"But that's true. You don't comprehend how vicious and dangerous Roddy Pickfair can be."

"I do, but I've got you down as being pretty vicious yourself."

She leaned forward, resting her palms on her knees. "What did you come here for?"

"To round up the rest of the delightful folks who had anything to do with Beth Kittridge's death," he replied. "That includes Larry Knerr, China Vargas and *you*."

"Don't you understand what I've been saying? I was simply hired to play a part."

"Tell it to the judge."

"Is Cardigan here with you?"

"Why?"

"Just tell me if he went into the underground rooms hunting for his son."

Gomez frowned. "That was what he intended to—"

"You have to catch him and stop him, Gomez," she urged. "Roddy's set a trap for him."

Roddy Pickfair chuckled. "I'll be leaving you, kids, to keep my appointment with Cardigan," he told them. "This wallscreen will keep running so that you can follow the whole thing."

On the screen the figure of Jake was moving slowly along an underground corridor.

"In a way, I'll be sorry to kill him finally," admitted the pudgy young man. "This has provided me with a good deal of fun and amusement these past—"

"You can't!" shouted Dan. "I'm not going to let you kill my father." He broke away from Molly's grip.

The wall suddenly went blank. The lights in the room and in the hallway died. Darkness closed in and absolute silence.

"What's going on, you idiots?" cried Pickfair. "Switch to the emergency power system."

Then he made a pained grunting sound and something metallic hit the floor.

Light blossomed next to him.

"Dad!" said Dan, laughing.

Jake, grinning over at him, set the newly lit

electriclantern beside the crouched figure of Pickfair. "You okay? Both of you?"

"We're fine—but what are you doing in that Brazil Wars uniform?" Dan went hurrying over to him. "We were watching you on the screen and you were dressed differently."

"Get up, Roddy," suggested Jake.

The studio head remained crouched, rubbing at his wrist. "You used a decoy."

"Yep, that was an android performer named Jacko Fuller—made up to look like me," admitted Jake. "Gomez rented him. It's the first time he's worked in over a year."

"But you used China's electrokey to get into the facility. And we've been monitoring your progress ever since."

"I figured you would, which is why I sent in Jacko."

"Then how did you get—"

"Your security system isn't all that tricky. After I'd studied the plans for this place, I worked out a way to get in."

"And you're the one who turned off all the power?"

Jake nodded. "Get up and we'll get going—I have a lot of people to turn over to the law."

Very slowly, Pickfair rose to his feet.

Backing, Jake picked up the lazgun he'd knocked from the young man's hand.

Pickfair smiled faintly. "Go ahead and use that," he invited. "If you don't know already, your son can tell you. I'm the one who master-minded everything that's happened to you."

Jake hefted the gun on his palm. "A day or so ago I was burning up with this," he said quietly. "Hell, even an hour ago I was thinking about killing you once I found you." He stuck the gun into his belt.

"But now?"

Jake shook his head. "Now I don't feel a damn thing."

A week later it rained all across Greater LA. A chill heavy rain that went on and on.

Jake, alone, was walking along the midday beach near his home. His shoulders were hunched, his hands were thrust deep in his trouser pockets.

From the opposite direction a pretty young actress came running enthusiastically along the rainswept sand. "You're getting soaked," she commented as she jogged by him.

He didn't respond and kept walking.

A half a mile or so later, he halted and stood looking out at the choppy grey ocean.

"I'm touched," said someone behind him.

Jake turned. "Hi, Sid."

"Even a coldhearted, hardboiled old opera-tive such as me couldn't help but be moved by how forlorn you're looking, *amigo.*"

"I'm not after pity."

"Oh, so?"

"Did you want anything specific?"

"You haven't returned the chief's calls at all. You haven't returned mine for two days."

"I feel like being pretty much to myself."

"Dan's with you, isn't he?"

"Sure, but he understands."

"He has to pretend to, the poor kid's stuck with you for a *padre*," said Gomez. "The Cosmos Agency has a new case for us. It's an odd one *and* it apparently doesn't involve Tek at all. Why don't you come into the office with me this afternoon?"

He asked his friend, "You think I'm overdoing the mourning?"

"By about two or three days at least."

"Okay, I'll change and we'll go see what Bascom has to offer."

"Eventually," said his partner as they started back along the beach, "you can get over most things."

"Most things," said Jake.

Star Trek's *William Shatner* returns with the fifth novel in his popular Tek series.

WILLIAM SHATNER

author of *TekWar*

Tek Secret

Beautiful Alicia Bower, daughter of the world's wealthiest robotics industrialist, has disappeared. Though Alicia's family is not concerned, her boyfriend believes she is in great danger. He begins his own search, and turns to private investigator Jake Cardigan.

Lonely and bitter since the murder of the woman he loved, Cardigan is reluctant to respond. But with the encouragement of his trusted sidekick, Sid Gomez, Cardigan pursues the elusive socialite, and soon is caught up in a world of potentially deadly consequences.

Available in hardcover at bookstores everywhere.

G. P. Putnam's Sons
A member of The Putnam Berkley Group, Inc.